"Finn, it's getting late."

"I don't feel tired at all."

"We need our energy for climbing back down tomorrow," he said.

"Since we're coming back up here anyway, I've decided to stay."

"Stay? Oops!" A chunk of ice flew from beneath my ax and hit Uncle Stoppard in the chest.

"Wear your goggles," I said.

"Finn, don't you think—?"

CLANG!

I stopped chipping, breathless. "That was metal," I said.

Uncle Stoppard stared at me. "Yes, it was," he said slowly. "Metal, not snow." He pulled out his own walking ax and joined me. The ice and snow flew from beneath our axes as if it were attached by twin snow-blowers. The field between the ridges grew deep purple.

"Look at it!" I cried.

"I don't believe it," said Uncle Stoppard.

At the center of our minor excavation, a rough circle in the ice and snow, lay an ancient iron ring, as big as a doughnut. The doughnut was attached to a door.

**BE SURE TO READ EVERY
FINNEGAN ZWAKE MYSTERY:**

THE
VIKING
C · L · A · W

A FINNEGAN ZWAKE MYSTERY

MICHAEL DAHL

SIMON PULSE
New York London Toronto Sydney Singapore

First Simon Pulse edition November 2002
Text copyright © 2001 by Michael Dahl
First Archway edition July 2001

SIMON PULSE
An imprint of Simon & Schuster
Children's Publishing Division
1230 Avenue of the Americas
New York, NY 10020

Printed in USA

10 9 8 7 6 5 4

ISBN 978-1-4424-3101-0

To my two gorgeous sisters,
Linda and Melissa

Many thanks to my far-seeing and enthusiastic agents, Eric Alterman and Mark Ryan, and to my editor, Ingrid van der Leeden, for her deft expertise and dazzlingly resourceful mind. Also, thanks to David Frank for sharing his extensive Viking library; Louann Smith, of the Northtown Central Library in Blaine, Minnesota, for supplying me with forensic info; Kathy Baxter and Riley Harrison for wandering through the Reykjavik airport and buying me Icelandic candy bars; Jim Fairburn for knowing his way around a European flight deck; and Danny Thomas for climbing Thor's Mountain by rough draft.

1
Thor's Mountain

Ping, ping.

Uncle Stoppard tightened his seat belt. He turned to me and said, "That's the five-thousand-foot signal."

Through the plane window I saw a vast field of greenish-blue water. We were descending over the Atlantic Ocean. I squashed my face against the clear plastic and stretched my eyeballs to get a glimpse of our destination. A brown shore of jagged jigsaw pieces was rushing toward us. Farther away the sun was rising over dark, sharp-edged mountains. Volcano country.

"You should put that away," said Uncle Stoppard. "If we have a bumpy landing, those papers will fly all over the cabin."

He was referring to my journal. Ever since we took off from the Minneapolis airport, six hours ago, I had held the journal on my lap. It was my dad's idea. Like father, like Finn, says Uncle Stop.

Last year I had discovered my dad's journal in Uncle Stoppard's storage room in the basement. It had been sitting down there for the past eight years, ever since Mom and Dad had dropped me off with Uncle Stop before they flew to Iceland, hunting for

the Haunted City of Tquuli. You say it *too-cool-ee.*
Maybe you read about my parents' expedition; it was
written up in *Peephole* magazine. Legends say that
Tquuli is the site of a lost Viking colony hidden
somewhere in the mountains of Iceland. On the
slope of one of those mountains, the Thorsfell, my
parents' footprints ended abruptly in a field of new
snow. Just ended! When I first started living with
Uncle Stoppard, I would think about those footprints
and my parents all the time. Now I only think about
them every day.

My parents went searching for Tquuli because
they were archeologists. I mean, *are* archeologists. I
mean, both. Both are both. They're considered
legally dead since they've been missing so long, but
they're still alive. Don't ask me how I know, I just
know.

Dad kept a detailed record in his journal of the
archeological digs he and my mom worked on
around the world. I thought it would be a good idea
to keep my own record of everything that happens to
me and Uncle Stoppard in Iceland. So far my journal
has maps of Iceland, articles from newspapers about
mountain climbing, copied sections of library books
on footprints, fingerprints, and physical evidence. The
Peephole magazine article about the Zwake-Tquuli
expedition is taped to the front three pages. I practi-
cally have it memorized. The most important (and
weirdest) paragraphs come near the end of the article:

Two weeks after radio contact had failed for
the fifth time, a second expedition was
launched. Its mission was to discover not Tqu-

uli, but the missing Zwake party, and time was of the essence. Winter had arrived in the north Atlantic, dropping the temperatures well below zero. Expert trackers from Reykjavik and Myvatn retraced Anna and Leon Zwake's route up the sloping side of Thor's Mountain. Luckily, no rain or snow had fallen since the Americans had last radioed their friends from the famous volcano cone. . . .

A black-and-white photo shows the extinct volcano Thorsfell, Thor's Mountain: a massive black triangle with snow covering the upper half. Thor was the ancient god of thunder and lightning. In the comics he has long blond hair and looks like a member of the World Wrestling Federation. The ancient Icelanders thought Thor lived inside the mountain since the volcano flashed and rumbled like a thunderstorm. A caption below the photo says: *Thorsfell, the Fujiyama of the Vikings.* Fujiyama is a famous mountain in Japan. I guess the two mountains look alike.

The next paragraphs still spook me when I read them:

. . . On the third day of the expedition, the Icelandic trackers found the Zwake camp. Tents were empty, but there was no sign of panic or trouble. Sleeping bags were neatly laid out. Food sat abandoned on cold, tin dinner plates. A man's pipe was found tipped on its side, resting on a small camping table, as if it shortly expected its owner to return. No sign of the American archeologists anywhere.

Except for a pair of footprints in the snow.

The footprints, the only ones found at the site, are believed to have belonged to the Zwakes since they begin at their tent. The prints then leave the site, heading up the steep slope in a straight line. As the prints approach the base of a flat, smooth cliff wall, known locally as Thor's Navel, they vanish. There are no other prints nearby, nor any disturbances in the smooth, month-old snow. The trackers said it looked as if the Zwakes had been lifted up into the air.

No explanation exists for the bizarre disappearance of Anna and Leon Zwake. Or for the disappearance of the other four members of their party. The Zwake Tquuli Expedition will be listed in future history books along with the unknown fates of Amelia Earhart, D. B. Cooper, and the crew of the *Marie Celeste*.

Lifted up into the air. Helicopters? UFOs? In a few days I'd be standing and staring at Thor's Navel with my own eyes. Not a photo, but the real deal. I could check out for myself what had happened on that snowy slope, solve the riddle of my parents' bizarre disappearance.

Minneapolis is one of the few places in the world that has nonstop flights to Iceland. Our flight was on time and smooth, and every seat was full. I've decided that my favorite spot on the plane is the rest room. It's like sitting in your own private space capsule with a sink and toilet paper. When you flush, your ears pop. I had to check out all three of them.

The attendants were great, too. They brought me and

Uncle Stoppard all the free pop we wanted. Before they served dinner, they handed us tiny hot towels rolled up tight like eggrolls. I used mine to wipe the smudges off the little plastic window next to my seat.

"The towels are for your face," Uncle Stoppard whispered.

"I already washed my face three times," I whispered back.

After writing in my journal about the rest rooms, the windows, and the boring magazines, I nodded off for a few hours, half thinking, half dreaming. *Peephole* had featured photos of the four scientists who worked (and disappeared) with my parents. Their black-and-white faces bobbed in my brain like the ice cubes in my soda-pop glass. I could hear their clinking Icelandic names: Gunnar Gunnarson, Helga Johansdottir, Hallur Bjorklund, Hrolf Magnusson. Johansdottir sounded like "John's daughter." Minnesota was crammed full of Johnsons and Andersons and Carlsons. No Carlsdaughters.

Uncle Stoppard spent an hour up in the cockpit. American airlines don't allow passengers into the cockpit, but Icelandic planes do, so Uncle Stoppard finally got to ask a real live pilot some questions he had about flying. He's working on a new mystery—that's what Uncle Stoppard does, writes mysteries—called *Dead Air*. The whole story takes place inside an airplane during its flight. His villain stuffs a dead body into a carry-on bag and shoves it into an overhead compartment. Throughout our flight, I noticed Uncle Stoppard's cucumber-green eyes darting up at the compartments above our seats. Whenever he did, I would say, "How tall are you again, Uncle Stoppard? Six one, six two?"

"Don't worry, Finn. I'm not going to climb inside them."

He'd better make his dead body a short one.

An elderly woman wearing a fuzzy pink sweater and a cowboy hat left her seat, tapped Uncle Stoppard's shoulder, and asked for his autograph. She happened to be carrying a paperback edition of his best-selling thriller, *Into My Grave.*

"Is this your charming son?" she asked.

"Uh, no, this is my nephew," said Uncle Stoppard.

Why don't people who buy books *read* them? My name is right there on the inside back cover of her book. You can't miss it. Uncle Stoppard's photo (which I took in our apartment) accompanies my name in the blurb. It reads:

Stoppard Sterling is the author of five previous mysteries, including *Cold Feet, Cold on the Carpet, Cold Shoulders, Cold Cuts,* and *Sneezing and Coffin.* Mr. Sterling is a two-time winner of the Minnesota Book Award for Best Mystery, and received the Ruby Raven award for *Into My Grave* for World's Greatest Mystery Novel. He lives in Minneapolis where he is a part-time runner and full-time uncle to his nephew, Finnegan Zwake.

See? Finnegan Zwake. The last words. Uncle Stoppard says the last words in a sentence are always the most important.

I'm surprised people who meet us think I'm Uncle Stop's charming son. To look at us, you wouldn't think we were related. He's tall and muscular, I'm short and slender. He has green eyes, red hair, and a long nose (Uncle Stoppard calls it *aquiline*). I have light brown hair, pale skin, and freckles. Uncle Stoppard tells me I have a *mochachino* mop, *java* eyes, and a *triple latte* complexion with *nutmeg* sprinkles. Uncle Stoppard likes using big words. He also drinks a lot of coffee.

Our plane made its final approach to the runway. I looked out the window, trying to guess which one of those distant mountains was Thorsfell. Were the footprints still there? Had snow or wind over the last eight years eroded them from sight? I'll be able to find them even if no one else can see them. I know I will.

Good thing I listened to Uncle Stoppard and tucked my journal under the seat in front of me. The landing gear struck the runway with a bump, just as he had predicted. At that same moment, though, Uncle Stoppard decided to take a breath mint. The mints burst out of their box, and out of Uncle Stop's hands, like a wintergreen supernova. A few of them disappeared straight up his *aquiline* region. For the next few minutes I was busy picking mints off angry and startled passengers while Uncle Stoppard made weird snorting sounds into his handkerchief.

Inside the Reykjavik airport Uncle Stoppard continued to breathe out breath mints as we gathered our luggage off a conveyor belt and headed for the main doors. Luckily, our expedition supplies had been shipped ahead last month, right before school ended for the summer, and were stored at our hotel. We only had a few bags to carry through the lobby.

Before we reached the doors, however, a tall man in a blue suit approached us. "Mr. Stoppard Sterling?" he asked.

Great, I thought. Another fan wanting an autograph, slowing us down.

Uncle Stoppard adjusted his shoulder bag. "Yes," he said. "May I help you?"

The tall man noticed my purple sweatshirt. "Ah, Minnesota Vikings," he said, chuckling. "If you like real Vikings, you've come to the right place."

The man looked like a big-time actor in Hollywood. You know, one who plays either the good guy or the president. His thick, caramel-brown hair was the same color as his suntan. He had crinkles around his eyes, a nose like Uncle Stoppard's (but not nearly as minty fresh), and lots of perfect white teeth.

He had a strong handshake, too.

"I'm Ruben Roobick," said the man.

"Of Roobick's Cubes?" I said.

The man's eyebrows shot up. "You've heard of me." Who hasn't heard of the famous Ruben Roobick? The Ice Cube King. His blue Roobick's Cubes, sold in grocery stores all over America, are the best ice cubes in the world. Even pop that loses its fizz tastes better when a couple of the famous blue cubes are dropped in a glass. Our refrigerator back home has a blue Roobick's package sitting in the freezer.

"Pleased to meet you," said Uncle Stoppard.

Roobick's Cubes sponsors mountain-climbing expeditions all over the world, looking for new brands of ice for their customers. A few articles on Mr. R. and his climbing adventures were stuffed somewhere in my journal. That's probably why he was in Iceland.

"I've read all your books, Stoppard. May I call you

Stoppard? But I must confess," said Mr. Roobick with a wink, "that I always figure out who the killer is before your detective does. My wife says I should write my own mystery. Maybe you can give me some tips during the next few weeks."

Uncle Stoppard looked puzzled. "Uh, next few weeks?" he said.

The Ice Cube King grinned. "We'll be seeing a lot of each other during the next two weeks. I understand you're joining my little expedition to Thor's Mountain."

2
Blood in the Ice

"Your expedition?" sputtered Uncle Stoppard.

"He means *our* expedition," said a blond, spiky-haired man walking up to join Mr. Roobick. No, it was a woman. A muscular woman, with a caramel suntan, dazzling blue eyes, broad shoulders, and a wispy blond mustache. She gripped Uncle Stoppard's hand in a brisk handshake. "Glad to meet you, Stoppard," she said. "I'm Kate Roobick." She nodded her head toward the Ice Cube King. "This big lug's wife."

"And vice president of Roobick's Cubes," added her husband.

"And his climbing partner," said Kate.

Ruben Roobick chuckled again. "This gal has saved my butt up in the Rockies more times than I care to count. Ever climb in Yosemite, Stoppard?"

"You—you're both climbing Thor's Mountain?" asked Uncle Stoppard.

"Not alone," said Kate. She introduced the third member of their party. A tall, pretty woman with long red hair tied in a ponytail.

"Hi, Mr. Sterling, I love your books," said the woman. "I'm Sarah O'Hara. Mrs. Roobick's assistant."

"The woman who saves *my* butt," said Kate.

Sarah turned to me. "You must be the famous Finnegan Zwake."

My ears felt hot. "My parents were, I mean, *are* the famous ones."

Sarah nodded. "That's why you're going up the Thorsfell, right?"

"The Zwake Curse," Roobick said. "Everyone's read about it."

"I don't believe in curses," I said.

"Good for you," said Kate. "Neither do I. It's a bunch of flimflam made up by busybody reporters and superstitious minds."

"I don't know what I believe," Sarah said. "Iceland is a stranger country than I expected. The people here believe all kinds of things: giants, elves, ghosts ..."

"I believe in hard work," Roobick said. "How about you, Stoppard?"

Uncle Sterling still looked puzzled. "How did you know we were coming? And that we were climbing up Thor's Mountain?"

"Thorsfell," corrected Kate. "Get used to the Icelandic name."

"We heard about you and young Zwake from the Hockey Puckeys," Roobick said. He and his wife laughed.

"The what?" I asked.

Uncle Stoppard crinkled his cucumber eyes. "The Jokkipunki brothers. The fellows I hired to guide us up Thor's, uh, the Thorsfell."

"I believe their name is actually pronounced *yolky punky*," said Kate. "You know, like egg yolk."

"Hockey Puckey is just our little joke," said Roobick.

"Our little *yolk*," said Kate, then the two of them burst into laughter again.

"If Uncle Stoppard hired them," I said, "how could they—?"

"We're all going up the same mountain," Kate said. "You're looking for dead Vikings, we're looking for new ice-cube flavors."

"Safety in numbers," Sarah agreed softly.

"We're not looking for dead Vikings," I said. "We're looking for live archeologists. Two of them."

"I thought there were *six* members of the Zwake party," Sarah said.

I hardly ever thought about those people with the clinky names who had worked with my parents. Should I? Their footprints did not end in a field of snow, but they had vanished all the same. Thor's Navel. Four other archeologists. I wonder if any of them had kids.

"Expeditions do this all the time," Roobick explained. "Join forces. Like the Americans and Russians in outer space."

"And the Jokkipunki brothers make twice as much money for the same amount of work," Stoppard said grimly.

Roobick boomed out a laugh, showing off his perfect white teeth. "Can't blame them for wanting to make a buck," he said. "It's the American way. Besides, they didn't want to say no to either of us."

Kate nodded. "They're killing two birds with one stone."

Killing?

Uncle Stoppard and I found out that the Roobicks and Sarah O'Hara were staying at the same hotel in Reykjavik that we were. Mr. Roobick looked surprised. He must have glanced at Uncle Stop's jeans and sneaks and old bomber jacket and figured we weren't Hotel Puffin material. Not all millionaires wear suits and ties.

One weird thing happened before we left the airport. As we walked outside to find a taxicab on the street, I noticed a kid staring at us. He looked like he was my age, maybe fourteen or fifteen, had freckles, red hair, and glasses. He wore an orange warm-up jacket and jeans, just like an American teenager. At first I thought he was staring at something behind me, then I realized it was me. His beady blue eyes burned a hole into my brain. He was studying me, memorizing me, as if my face was going to be the answer on a final exam. I opened my mouth to speak, then he spun around and disappeared into the terminal.

"Who was that boy?" asked Uncle Stoppard, plopping his suitcases at the curb.

"You saw him, too?" I said. "Do I have a breath mint sticking out of my nose or something?"

"Maybe he wanted an autograph from the famous Finnegan Zwake."

Yeah, right. Whoever the strange kid in the orange jacket was, he was not a fan. His hard ice-blue eyes told me that much.

Reykjavik, the capital of Iceland, reminded me of Lego buildings. Everything is sharp, flat, and square. The short buildings, only two or three stories, are painted snow white, mouse gray, or crayon brown. The streets are wiped clean. They probably use those hot little towels from their airplanes. Even the grass in the park looked like it was vacuumed each night. Swans floated on a park pond like white chunks of soap. The most colorful thing in the city is the sky, big and bright and as blue as a gigantic Roobick's Cube. Uncle Stoppard told me that Reykjavik has no air pollution. The clean, glowing air made the mountains east of the city look as if they were next door instead of a hundred miles away.

Our cab drove past the first tall building I'd seen, a tower of gray brick shaped like a rocket with a small white cross on top. A greenish-blue statue of a guy in boots stood on a block of stone. He wore a helmet and carried a monster ax.

"A famous fireman, huh?" I asked.

"That's the man who discovered America," our cab driver said proudly. "That's Leifur Eiriksson."

I think he meant Leif Ericsson. I wanted to tell the cab driver that according to my history teacher America was discovered by mammoth hunters from Mongolia, but I didn't want to hurt his feelings. It was a cool statue. The ax—I had read something about an ax.

The Hotel Puffin had big metal puffins flanking the main doors. The lobby was decorated with hundreds of the stubby black birds with the orange beaks. A young guy at the front desk, in a puffin-orange tie, told us the maids were still cleaning our room, so we parked ourselves on fuzzy orange sofas in the lobby. I pulled my journal out of my shoulder bag and flipped through the notes. Where had I seen the word *ax* before?

Before Mom and Dad had flown to Iceland, they had done some research on the Haunted City of Tquuli. Dad wrote down a few notes, which I had copied from his journal into mine:

TQUULI or TQÚLÍ—legendary city of Viking dead

Graveyard? Burial for some Viking chief-
tain or princess?

Tales of warrior named Ogar Blueaxe
forcing his men to carry a ship up the
side of Thorsfell, burying it in a hidden city named Tquuli, hiding a treasure of Italian gold from his enemies

Did Ogar make up the story of the
Haunted City to scare away potential
thieves?

Thirteen men went up the Thorsfell, only
Ogar and his friend Skuld returned—
—did they kill the others to hide location of the treasure?
—or were they killed by ghosts of the
Haunted City?

Legends say that Ogar was renamed Redaxe
after his return from Thorsfell.

Ogar might have killed eleven of his shipmates to
keep them from blabbing where the treasure boat
was buried. Eleven friends cold as ice. Now the blade
of the blue ax was a permanent bloodred. People do
a lot of stupid things to get rich. Answer questions on
game shows. Live on a desert island with a bunch of
loopy strangers. Kill people.

Would people kill for a treasure that hadn't been
seen in over ten centuries?

Sarah O'Hara sat across from me in the lobby. She
was waiting for Mrs. Roobick to come back from the
ladies' room so they could go to breakfast. The Ice
Cube King was telling Uncle Stoppard to join them
at a nearby restaurant. My stomach growled.

Sarah was leafing through her own journal. Earlier

she had asked me about the other archeologists who worked with my parents. Had my parents and their teammates discovered the boatload of gold left behind by Ogar Blueaxe? And had members of the Zwake party been permanently silenced in order to keep the treasure a secret? That was one explanation for the mass disappearance. Maybe one of the missing archeologists was enjoying his stolen wealth on some faraway Pacific island, slurping drinks on a remote beach where he would never be discovered or arrested.

The *Peephole* article said that the trackers who found the deserted Zwake camp found no signs of "panic or trouble." In other words, no blood. No struggle with an ax, real or ghostly. No evidence of murder. Even if there had been signs of trouble, murder still did not explain those chopped-off, er, interrupted footprints.

A blur of orange caught the corner of my eye. That kid from the airport. He was walking through the lobby in his orange warm-up jacket. When he reached the front desk, about twenty feet away from where I sat, he turned and stared at me again. His red hair, slanty eyes, and sharp cheekbones reminded me of a fox. The guy in the puffin tie appeared at the desk. The fox turned and sprinted away.

I jumped up to follow him. My journal spilled from my lap, pages fluttering all over the white tiled floor.

"I'll help," said Sarah. "That's happened to me once or twice."

When I looked up, the kid in the orange jacket was gone.

Mr. Roobick's big laugh echoed through the lobby. Was he laughing at my mess? No, he was talking to

Uncle Stoppard, clapping his hand on my uncle's shoulder. I could tell Uncle Stop didn't like it.

"Thanks for helping," I said to Sarah as we knelt on the tiles, assembling all my loose pages and notes.

"No problem," she said, smiling. Her smile froze into a thin line. She was holding one of the newspaper articles I had collected on mountain climbing. She shoved it into my hands. "No problem," she said again, sharper this time. She stood up and walked toward the women's rest room.

People say *no problem* when there usually is a problem.

The newspaper clipping she handed me began with the words BOLIVIAN ICE-CUBE EXPEDITION ENDS IN TRAGEDY. Two years ago Roobick's Cubes had sent a team of ice explorers to the mountains surrounding Lake Poopo in Bolivia. One of the team members had fallen twenty feet into a crevasse, headfirst, and got stuck upside-down. He died while his friends tried to rescue him. Roobick's Cubes named a flavor after him, Gomez Guava.

Since Sarah O'Hara worked for the Roobicks, maybe she knew the climber who died. That would explain her acting upset.

Roobick laughed again. He laughs a lot. He laughed that same way at the airport when he said the Jokkipunki brothers were only trying to make a buck by guiding a double expedition. Killing two birds with one stone.

I wonder if the Jokkipunkis ever had a friend who got stuck in a crevasse and died. Did they see worse tragedies? If they had, it didn't stop them from climbing. Guys who make their living scrambling up the sides of icy cliffs have to be fearless. Rock cowboys, Uncle Stoppard calls them, daredevils.

Would the Hockey Puckeys dare anything for extra money—or for Viking gold? Would they kill five birds with one stone?

My stomach grumbled and my eyes burned. Jet lag. That's why I was thinking these creepy thoughts about red axes and murder and treacherous gold hunters. I had never even met the Jokkipunki climbers. They were probably nice guys.

I still planned to keep my eyes peeled for anyone on the expedition carrying an ax.

3
The Boiling Boy

"Everyone carries an ax," said Teemu Jokkipunki. "It is your best friend on the mountain."

"Your second-best friend," added his brother Edo. "Your best friend is us. Follow our instructions and you'll avoid a lot of problems. My brother and I have made the trek up the Thorsfell at least five times."

Straight as a Viking spear, the highway stretched its gray line through the glowing green countryside, while Teemu at the wheel, and Edo standing in the doorwell, drove us in their minibus toward the ever-expanding shadow of the Thorsfell. We had met the Jokkipunki brothers for lunch yesterday, our first day in Iceland. Their plan was to drive us to the base of the mountain, go to bed early, and begin climbing first thing in the morning. Our camping and climbing gear was bungee-corded to the roof of the minibus.

You could easily see the Hockey Puckeys were brothers. Both were young, brown-haired, suntanned, and cheerful. Both Jokkipunki brothers were shorter than Sarah O'Hara by two to three inches. Size doesn't matter when you're climbing a mountain, I guess, as long as you have powerful arms and legs. If you don't weigh much, maybe you won't hit the ground as hard when you fall.

Edo had thick eyebrows—black, velvety bandages. Teemu had a dark, devilish goatee. Finnish pit bulls, Uncle Stoppard called them. Born in Finland, the Jokkipunkis moved to Iceland to live with their cousins. Yesterday at lunch, Teemu had shaken my hand and joked, "You'll be a good climber. You're a Finn like us." Ha ha.

Both brothers had bone-crushing grips, like Ruben Roobick. Years of mountaineering had given them stronger muscles in their fingers and toes than I had in my whole body. Their loose-fitting nylon jackets and trousers hid their muscles, but you could see the strength in their thick necks whenever they turned to look out the minibus window.

I gazed out the window and watched the empty countryside. I had already heard Edo (or was it Teemu?) tell me how important an ice ax was at least a dozen times since yesterday afternoon. Walking axes would be strapped around each climber's wrist with a nylon cord. If we felt ourselves sliding down the lava or snow slopes of Thorsfell, we were instructed to turn on our side, grip the ax against our chest, and drive the pointed end into the rock slipping past us. The ax would, hopefully, stick in the rock or ice, and slow us down. During the day-to-day climb, our ax would serve as an extra support. It was just tall enough to lean on. I hoped Ogar Blueaxe or Redaxe or his pal Skuld weren't planning a ghostly raid during our climb. That's all we needed: a phantom ax murderer with an arsenal of modern, high-tech weapons to choose from.

From the moment the minibus pulled out of Reykjavik that morning, I jotted notes in my journal. I followed each turn of the route with my finger tracing a map Uncle Stoppard had bought me back at the Mall of America. I also followed along by reading the *Peephole* article's description of the trail to Thorsfell:

> "Vast green fields contain massive moss-covered boulders, resembling a game of marbles recently abandoned by Norse giants. . . ."

I looked out the window. Yup, mossy marbles.

> "Beyond the boulders loomed a brownish, bleak, volcanic landscape. An otherworldly, almost Martian vista of cold and gloom . . ."

The minibus chugged upward, winding through a vista of grassy hills. Mr. Roobick joked that the countries of Greenland and Iceland should exchange names. "Good one," said Kate. Then I heard him complain to his wife about the ice cubes at the hotel. "No flavor, no color. They might as well have been plastic. I hope that's not a sign of things to come."

The passing green hills gleamed like emeralds. Grass everywhere, but no trees.

"What do you do if you are lost in an Icelandic forest?" Edo asked me.

"I don't know."

"Stand up!" He laughed.

Herds of ghostly sheep glided up and down the steep hills. One sheep vanished into the air. Then two more.

"Hey, that sheep!" I cried. "Where did it go?"

"The vapor comes from hot springs," Edo explained, leaning over my seat. Edo's smile was as big as his bushy eyebrows. "Iceland is full of geysers and mudholes and volcanic springs."

Those sheep were vapor?

Edo glanced at his massive watch, studded with knobs and dials. "How much longer, Teemu?"

"Fimm," said Teemu.

Edo held up his fingers to me and smiled. "That's five minutes." He went over to the next seat and asked Sarah, "Have I explained the harness to you yet?" He sat close to her. Real close. Teemu, at the wheel, turned his head and watched them.

Not far from the road, a geyser of steam shot fifty feet into the air. Everyone in the van murmured "Oooooohh" as if it was fireworks.

Edo stood up from his seat and donned his sunglasses. "This is it."

Teemu parked the minibus on the side of the two-lane asphalt road.

"This is not the mountain," complained Kate Roobick.

"This is the middle of nowhere," said Sarah nervously.

Roobick nodded. "It's only noon," he said to Edo. "I thought you told me we wouldn't reach the base camp until four o'clock."

Teemu smiled through his dark goatee as he opened the bus door. He swept his long brown hair behind his ears. "This is, as you Americans say, a pit stop," he said.

I jumped down off the bus but didn't see any bathroom. Teemu wriggled past me and took Sarah's hand, helping her down the bus's front steps.

The wind tugged at the collar of my green-and-orange vinyl jacket. Edo saw me shivering. "You should be used to this kind of weather in Minnesota," he said, grinning.

"Not in July," I said. "This feels more like Halloween."

"Wait until we reach Thorsnafli," he said. "It will feel like true winter."

"At least there are no mosquitoes in Iceland," said Uncle Stoppard, zipping up his nylon jacket. "I think the cold kills them off."

"Looks like a farm over there," I said. A small white house, about a mile from the road, perched on a green slope dotted with yellow freckles. Our first sight of flowers.

"Over here!" shouted Teemu. "Out of the wind." He stood in a small gully next to the road, on the side away from the farm. As we followed close behind him, the path slanted deeper into the hillside. Gray and red boulders thrust upward through the grass. The sides of the trail grew into walls on either side of us. The blazing blue sky, glimpsed overhead between the walls of rock, reminded me of the same blue sky Uncle Stoppard and I had seen when we visited the Sahara last October. The wind gusting across the lip of the gully, raining gravel on my head, reminded me I was in Viking country. My face and ears were cold, but my feet felt warm. Volcanic springs? Just as my feet started getting hot, the trail was replaced by a boardwalk of wooden planks.

"Exactly where are we going?" demanded Kate.

The boardwalk zigzagged through the reddish rock. I heard a friendly cry up ahead. A splash! There were no lakes or rivers nearby according to my map. From the minibus's windows, all I had seen around us were miles and miles of grassy hillside. Another splash.

The trail opened up on either side of us, widening

out into a huge bowl of rock shielded from the wind and cold. A flinty ledge ran around the rim of the bowl, circling a steaming pool of green, boiling water. In the center of the hot spring, half hidden by sheep-sized vapor clouds, was a boiling, grinning boy, his skin as wet and red as a lobster. His foxy eyes were hard chips of blue ice. He wasn't wearing his orange jacket—in fact, he wasn't wearing anything, not even his glasses—but I recognized him as the kid from the airport and the hotel lobby.

Teemu and Edo stripped down to their underwear. "This is a good relax before our climb," said Edo. "Come on down!" He cannonballed into the green pool. Sarah giggled as the spray hit us. Teemu waded in after his brother. He kept flexing his suntanned arms like he was stretching, but I think he was showing off his muscles.

I looked at Uncle Stoppard. "Well," he said. "When in Rome." We weren't in Rome, but I knew what he meant. Mr. and Mrs. Roobick started unlacing their shoes. Sarah pulled off her nylon jacket and pants. Americans, especially Minnesotans, aren't used to this kind of thing. The Zwake-Roobick expedition still retained a few articles of clothing. When Sarah stepped cautiously into the water, a smile spread across her face. "Mmmm, feels wonderful," she said.

"It is called the Witch's Cauldron," said Edo.

Our eccentric landlady, Ms. Pryce, who sometimes wears a skull belt buckle with her all-black wardrobe, would feel right at home here. The green cauldron bubbled and steamed like a scene from a Halloween movie. Now I knew why the red-headed teenager had removed his glasses; mine were covered with a misty film.

The warm water, level with my chin, tasted tangy and bitter. Uncle Stoppard sat with his eyes closed, a dreamy expression on his face. His red hair was wet, plastered flat against his skull. I was trying to figure out how I'd get my wet underwear off before I put my pants back on when we got up to leave.

"This was an excellent idea," said Kate to her husband, almost as if it were his idea.

I noticed Mr. Roobick's hairy chest was gray, not the same color as his wavy, caramel hair. He turned to the Jokkipunkis and said, "Are you going to introduce us to your little friend?"

The fox's ice-cube eyes grew sharp.

"This is our cousin Hrór," said Edo.

"Gothan dag," said Hrór. That means "hi" in Icelandic.

"Roar?" said Roobick. "Like a lion's roar?"

Edo pronounced the boy's name again, giving it a little breath at the beginning. "Hrór is a good, old-fashioned Viking name."

"His family lives on the farm across the road," added Teemu. "They moved here from Finland many years before we did. Hrór was born here."

"Mountains are in his blood," Edo said. "He's a great rock climber."

That kid?

Uncle Stoppard opened his eyes. "Do you mean that he's—?"

Hrór cleared his throat, then recited in perfect American:

Born in the mountains,
Climbing rocks since I was five,
I will come with you.

No one spoke.

"What the heck was that?" I asked.

"Haiku," muttered Uncle Stoppard.

"Yeah, I like you, too," I said. "But why did he talk like that?"

Then Edo chimed in:

Older and wiser,
Climbing before you were born,
I give the orders.

Everyone laughed, even Hrór. "We Icelanders love poetry," said Edo. "It is in our blood."

"Some of the world's greatest poems were written by Icelanders," said Hrór.

"Do you know *The Shooting of Dan McGrew*?" I asked. Now *there* was a poem.

"Uh, why haiku?" asked Uncle Stoppard. "I thought that was supposed to be popular in Japan. And I thought Icelanders preferred long, epic poems called sagas."

Edo shrugged his shoulders. "Poetry is poetry," he said.

"It's the new millennium," said Hrór.

I wonder if he does rap.

"Does his little haiku mean he's accompanying us?" asked Roobick.

"Another youngster?" said Kate. She looked at me, then quickly looked away.

"Hrór has climbed several times with us," replied Edo.

"Do you know ice as well as you know the mountains?" asked Roobick. "I need help finding another flavor for my product line."

"Not now, Ruben," said Kate, shaking her head. Water droplets hung from her faint blond mustache.

"Kids have better taste buds than old folks like us," said Roobick. "He's from Iceland, he should know ice. I'm counting on Finn, and Roar here, to tell me what kinds of ice the modern, new-millenium kids like."

No one told me I was going to be an official ice taster. Uncle Stoppard's mouth was set in a tight, grim line. It would be cool to see a new flavor of Roobick's Cubes in the grocery freezer, knowing that I had had a hand, or tongue, in helping the Ice Cube King discover it. But when would I have the time? I'd be too busy discovering my parents and solving the mystery of Thor's Belly Button.

Edo stood up, the water sliding down his red shoulders. Drops glistened on his velvet eyebrows. A sword tattoo gleamed on his chest above his heart, its yellow blade matching the yellow of his shorts. Edo caught sight of Sarah staring at him, and blushed. "Hrór and I will get his gear from the farm," he said. "We will meet you back at the bus in half an hour. Everyone, enjoy!" Hrór's clothes, orange jacket, and glasses had been stashed on the other side of the green pool. Edo changed into his nylon warm-up suit behind an outcropping of damp rock. When the two dressed cousins filed out through the narrow passageway, Roobick flashed his white teeth. "You can't pay for a better hot tub than this," he said, smiling.

Uncle Stoppard did not look relaxed.

"Are you okay?" I asked.

Was that a shout? Teemu's head shot up from the surface of the pool. He cocked his head. "That's Edo!" he cried.

A second shout echoed down the trail.

Teemu jumped onto the rocky ledge and yanked on his clothes without drying off. He was pulling on his boots when Hrór appeared, breathless, at the entrance to the passage.

"Edo," he said. "He sent me back. Something bad happened to the bus."

4
The Rat

One glance at the minibus and my heart instantly froze. All four tires were flat.

"What did you do?" yelled Teemu, when he emerged from the rocky gully. One after another, we had crawled or climbed out of the steaming cauldron, and struggled back into our clothes. I solved the problem of what to do with my wet underwear. I kept them on. Yuck! There was no time to change out of them. When we heard Hrór say something bad happened to the bus, our main goal was to reach the road as quickly as possible.

"I didn't do anything!" Edo yelled back at his brother. "It was like this when we got out here. Ask Hrór."

Hrór nodded vigorously.

On the lonely road
Our minibus was attacked.
Every wheel was flat.

"Do you have spares?" asked Roobick.

"Not four," said Edo. "We'll have to get these repaired back in town before we can go any farther."

"Someone did this," said Kate angrily. "Four tires don't go flat all by themselves!"

Teemu was bent over the back right tire. "This one's been cut!" he cried.

Wind blew across the two lanes. The noon sun blazed on the asphalt, a smooth black ribbon that stretched for miles in either direction. As far as we could see, there were no cars or other vehicles. Not even a lonely bicycle.

"Who could have done this?" asked Sarah.

"Sabotage!" said Roobick. "It's those blasted creeps from Ice Flo's. They're following me again. Like they did in South America. Spying on me, trying to beat me to a new ice flavor!"

Ice Flo's was named for Florence Waters, the Ice Cube Queen. Her small but aggressive company was Ruben Roobick's only rival in the frozen water market. Roobick's had better ice, but Flo's had better commercials.

"The important thing is not who did this, but what is our next step," Kate said. "Is there a car at Hrór's farm?"

"Ja," said Edo. "We will have to stay here overnight."

"Overnight?" I said.

Edo continued, "We need to take all four tires into town for repairs. This will set us back at least a day."

"A day!" I wailed.

"And the cost of new tires," Teemu tacked on.

Kate said to her husband, in a whisper we all could hear, "And the cost of an extra day's worth of guiding."

"We'll just have to walk," I said.

"Finn, we're not walking," said Uncle Stoppard.

"Yes, we are," I said. "Put one foot in front of the other ..."

"Finn."

"We can't stop now."

"One day," said Uncle Stoppard. "We've waited eight years. What's one more day?"

"Aren't the days like two months long up here?"

"That's in the Arctic Circle," he said, putting a hand on my shoulder.

"Close enough," I muttered. I really hate it when he's right.

"Should we unpack all of our stuff?" asked Uncle Stoppard.

"I'm afraid we'll have to," Edo said. "Under normal circumstances, I'd say leave it. The roads in Iceland are safe. This is not America. But if someone did cut our tires, they may come back for more mischief."

More mischief? Who would want to keep us from the mountain, unless Roobick was right and we were the victims of ice-cube industry sabotage.

Uncle Stoppard, Sarah, Hrór, and I climbed on top of the minibus and un-bungee-corded our gear. We handed the bags and cases down to the others, and Teemu locked the minibus. In a few minutes we were marching in a ragged line across the grassy fields toward the small white farmhouse. Uncle Stoppard's red head bobbed above the rest. My underwear squished at each step.

Hrór's family was warm and friendly, three grown-ups, a couple teenagers, and two kids younger than Hrór. The grown-ups were all short, like Edo and Teemu. They became alarmingly angry when E. and T. told them about the rats who wrecked our tires. Lots of shouts, angry words, fists in the direction of the road. I didn't understand what they were saying, but it wouldn't have surprised me if they had grabbed spears from their closets and raced off after our nameless attackers. Teemu and one of the older teenagers, a boy named Gisli, a real Viking with sharp cheekbones, golden hair, and shaggy sideburns, drove over to the minibus in a rusty old clunker.

Hrór's mom or older sister, I never learned which, herded the rest of us out of her small, neat house and led us to our sleeping quarters. Mrs. Hrór wore a long blue skirt and a thick red sweater. A big ring of keys jangled in her fist. We followed the back of her sweater through the waving grass to a large white building tucked into a fold of the hills, invisible from the highway.

When the mother, or sister, unlocked the huge door and we filed inside, Uncle Stoppard sniffed the moist air. "Cows?" he asked.

"Sheep," Edo said. "Sheep in the winter. In the summer the herd is grazing in the hills. We can sleep here tonight. We can put our sleeping bags on the straw."

"A big slumber party," said Sarah O'Hara.

Mrs. Hrór treated us to a huge dinner in her tiny kitchen. Bowls of steaming fish soup, red cabbage, candied potatoes, sausage, thick juicy lamb chops, and little cakes swimming in cream.

While we ate, Edo went around and introduced each of us to his family. When he got to Uncle Stoppard and said he was a famous mystery writer from Minneapolis, the sheep farmers were impressed.

Mrs. Hrór excitedly asked Edo a question in Icelandic. His velvety eyebrows went up and down. Edo turned to Uncle Stoppard and said, "Do you know Mona Trafalgar-Squeer?"

Unfortunately, Uncle Stoppard had just taken a spoonful of fish soup.

"I love her stuff," said Kate, nodding and smiling to Mrs. Hrór.

"*Ja, ja,* Mona," murmured the other Icelander grown-ups.

Uncle Stoppard wiped his face and quietly set his spoon in his bowl. "Yes," he said in a dangerous voice, "Ms. Squeer and I have met on occasion."

Met? Mona once helped me rescue Uncle Stoppard from a clever killer. For some reason, though, he and Mona never see eye to eye. Like Roobick and Flo Waters.

Mona Trafalgar-Squeer is the world's most stunning mystery writer. After Uncle Stoppard, of course. Critics and news reporters call her the Princess of Puzzles, the Diva of Deception, the Queen of Crime. Uncle Stoppard says it's a crime her books sell. Mona was born in England and is a British citizen, but she spends her summers in Minneapolis. Mystery fans have spotted her racing around the city streets on a giant silver Kawasaki.

Mona's always working on a new book. Her newest mystery came out last winter, *Cold to the Bone.* (Uncle Stoppard was not happy with Mona using the word *cold* in her title. He's already used it four times, and thinks she's copying him.) The villain in Mona's book, the wicked Duchess of DeMonica, kills her victims using a reverse microwave oven. People freeze to death from the inside out. One of the reverse-frozen bodies is found in a desert. Neat, huh? I have a copy of the book hidden in my backpack.

Mona's plots are the best—they're galactic. You

can never figure them out until the final page, or sometimes the final word. Uncle Stoppard thinks *Cold to the Bone* will get a cool reception from the critics.

"Care for a true Icelandic delicacy?" asked Edo. He handed Uncle Stoppard a plate covered with dark, flat wedges. Roof shingles? The two littlest Hrórs giggled.

"Looks interesting," said Uncle Stoppard.

"Pickled seal flipper."

Uncle Stoppard's complexion matched the color of his cucumber-green eyes. "Uh, I'd love to, but . . . um . . ."

"He's allergic to anything with whiskers," I said.

Edo translated our remarks for the little Hrórs, and they giggled even louder.

Throughout dinner Hrór asked me questions about American movies and rock music. He liked my sneakers. I told him about the Dan McGrew poem and the shoot-out at the Malamute Saloon. He even tried on my glasses; he's near sighted, too. Hrór never stared at me again the way he had at the airport or the Hotel Puffin. Maybe Uncle Stoppard was right— maybe Hrór thought I was someone else when he first saw me. But what had he been doing in both those places? I was warming up to asking him when Mrs. Hrór announced that dinner was over.

Uncle Stoppard and I offered to help clean up the dishes, like good Minnesotans, but Mrs. Hrór pushed us out of her kitchen.

The barn was warmer than I expected. In one of the corners we stacked old bales of hay on three sides, creating a small enclosure. Another Hrór teenager, a Viking princess in jeans and a red sweater like the older woman, brought us a lantern. Before she left the barn, the princess filled a basket with our wet clothes to take and hang over the kitchen stove during the night. I made sure my underwear was at the bottom of the basket. Edo lit the lantern with a match and set it on the well-swept floor. Our sleeping bags formed a circle around the softly glowing light.

"You were right," said Kate to Sarah, in the sleeping bag to her right. "This is a big slumber party."

"What time will Teemu return?" asked Roobick.

Edo frowned. "I think he will stay in the city until morning. He'll get the tires fixed as soon as the shops open, then he rejoins us."

"Might as well make the best of it," said Roobick. "I'm going to give that witch's bathtub another try in the morning."

I thought people would stay up and talk, but the warm food and fresh mountain air made us sleepy. Edo turned the lamp down. Soon I heard Uncle Stoppard's familiar snores rumbling on my left.

Hrór's snores were just as bad. Hrór's snores . . . that's funny. I came up with the first line of a haiku. *Hrór's snores were loud as boars.* I'd have to tell that one to Uncle Stoppard in the morning. My eyelids drooped. The sleeping bag felt as warm and welcome as the witch's green pool. So warm. The last thing I remember was stretching and wiggling my toes, feeling my journal, and Mona's book, safely tucked at the bottom of my bag.

CREEAK!

I sat up, blinking, and looked around in the dim lantern light. Six sleeping forms lay motionless. Where had that sound come from?

Silence.

The countryside was perfectly quiet. Then I heard a faint, faraway cry, sheep baaing on a distant hill. A dog barked somewhere. Nothing else, but the soft sounds of six people sleeping. No airplanes, no cars, no late-night television, no boom boxes driving by, vibrating our apartment windows.

Hrór's sleeping bag was empty. I quietly crawled over to check it out. Yeah, he was gone. Something white lay near his pillow. I didn't believe it! Hrór had been messing with my journal. The white object was a sheet of paper, a page ripped from the *Peephole* article on my missing parents. Wait a minute. It was the same article, but different. The words were in Icelandic.

Why was Hrór carrying around his own copy of the *Peephole?* Research on the expedition he'd be helping his cousins with?

There was that sound again. The second creak came from overhead. Rats. I heard something heavy slide along the wooden beam above the circle of sleeping bags. Big rats.

I crawled back to my bag. Tomorrow morning, I'll ask Hrór about that article. Or maybe I'll let him see me open my journal, or accidentally drop it at his feet, open to the same page he had half hidden under his pillow. See if Hrór says anything.

Slowly I lay down and closed my eyes. The rat was quiet now. I'd just ignore it.

I think I fell asleep. Crumbs of dust landed on my forehead and cheeks. There *was* something moving up there. I couldn't help myself. I brushed the dust off my face with my sleeve and opened my eyes.

Hanging above me on the wooden beam, reflected in the dim light of the lantern, was a face wearing a pair of black sunglasses.

5
Freya's Chariot

Uncle Stoppard was shaking my shoulders. "What's wrong, Finn?" he shouted.

"What? What?" I stuttered.

"You were mumbling," said Sarah. "Quite loudly." She was wide awake, along with the rest of the barn, sitting up in her sleeping bag, staring at me.

I pointed at the wooden beam overhead. "There," I said. "I saw someone up there. Someone wearing sunglasses."

Everyone followed my finger. Hrór was hanging upside down, his arms and legs wrapped around the beam like a red-headed koala bear.

Edo sighed. "He's been climbing in his sleep again," he said.

My own nearsightedness and the dim lantern confused me. In the murky light Hrór's glasses looked like sunglasses.

"He climbs in his sleep?" asked Kate.

Edo had risen from his sleeping bag. Teemu stood beneath the sleeping teenager, with his arms outspread. Edo was looking for a way to climb up.

"I thought he was an Ackerberg," I whispered to Uncle Stoppard.

"What would an Ackerberg be doing up there?"

"Spying on me."

"You were dreaming," said Uncle Stoppard. "All that talk of Roobick's about sabotage and spies gave you a nightmare."

Hrór's blue eyes popped open. He made a funny gurgling sound, then said, "Why are you guys up on the roof? *Uff da!*" He fell with a whoop into his cousin's arms.

Edo laughed and ruffled Hrór's hair.

"Here are your glasses, Hrór," said Kate. She picked them up from where they had fallen onto her sleeping bag.

"Was it something the young man ate?" asked Roobick with a yawn.

Maybe it was the pickled seal flipper.

"He has done this before," said Edo. "He has the mountains in his blood. We need to watch him when we get up on the cliffs." Then he added:

Climbing in the dark,
The red fox forgets one thing:
He needs his glasses.

"And he needs his sleep," Kate said.

Hrór's face was red. He flashed a crooked grin and then dived into his bag.

Edo turned the lamp back down and returned to his bag, too. I climbed back into mine, shivering, and leaned over to Uncle Stoppard. "Ackerberg," I whispered.

Uncle Stoppard shook his head slowly. "You have enough on your mind during this trip without worrying about them," he said. The mysterious Ackerberg

Institute had hired my parents years ago and sent them on various archeological digs, including the one to Tquuli. Uncle Stoppard and I had met the agents of the Institute a few times: men who wore black suits, black gloves, and black sunglasses even at night. I had always wondered if they knew the truth behind my parents' disappearance, but there was no way to get in touch with them. No one knew where the Ackerberg Institute was located. They had a Web site, but they had never returned any of my e-mail.

"Then what about the tires?" I demanded.

"You think the Ackerbergs did that?" he asked.

"Who else?"

Uncle Stoppard darted his eyes around the sleeping bag circle. "I looked at the rips in the rubber," he whispered. "It was no accident. Something sharp made those holes."

"An ax?"

"Something smaller than an ax."

"A little ax?"

"You have axes on the brain."

"You don't think it was the Ackerberg guys?" I said.

"Where did they come from? There were no other cars around."

"Black copters," I said.

"In a clear blue sky?"

"Then maybe Roobick's right. Maybe it was a spy from Ice Flo's."

Uncle Stoppard glanced around at the sleepers again. "That's what I'm not sure about," he said. "It seems odd that someone would attack the minibus while we made an unscheduled stop in the middle of the empty countryside."

"Not totally empty," I said. "This farm is here."

"Exactly," said Uncle Stoppard grimly. "The farm."

"You think one of those nice farm people did it?"

"Or someone sleeping in this barn did it."

I fell asleep trying to remember who was the last person to reach the Witch's Cauldron. Who was at the back of the line?

Brilliant morning sunlight poured through the barn door. During the night, Uncle Stoppard had somehow managed to turn completely around inside his sleeping bag. His stocking feet stuck out the top like a pair of skis. When he woke up, he thought the barn had collapsed on him.

A whiff of sizzling sausage tickled my nose. We rolled up our sleeping bags and pulled on our shoes and boots. Hrór and I were the last ones out of the barn.

"Can I ask you something?" I said.

"Ja," said Hrór.

"How did you climb up there last night? It looked pretty cool."

"Easy," said Hrór. "The hay."

The bales of hay formed a perfect staircase. I climbed to the top of the far wall, where the beam met the sloping roof. The beam hung two feet above my head. I gripped it with my fingers (the months of rock climbing paid off), pulled myself up, then lay along the length of the beam.

"You did that pretty easy," said Hrór.

"Uncle Stop and I have been rock climbing back home," I said. "I figured we'd better practice before we tackled the Thorsfell."

"There are mountains in Minnesota?" he asked.

"No, but we have the Mall of America."

"Ah."

"And they have a rock-climbing wall."

"Very cool," Hrór said. "In America you can shop while you climb."

The beam was only a foot wide. Dust and straw and chalky-white bird doo littered the top surface. I sat up, hanging a leg over each side.

"See? It was easy," said Hrór.

"You must have been dreaming about climbing."

"*Ja,* all the time." Funny. Hrór didn't sound all that excited when he said that.

I scooted myself along the beam, trying to avoid slivers in my jeans. The sleeping bags were rolled up like hot little towels below me.

I was about to jump down when I saw a shoeprint in the thick layer of dust. Hrór's sneakers. Another print lay just beyond the first. Then a third. The footprints ended abruptly, directly above my sleeping bag.

Ending like those other footprints in the snow on Thor's Mountain.

The mystery of Hrór's prints was easier to solve. Hrór had simply jumped, or rather fallen, off the beam. Fallen down. *Down?* That gave me an idea.

"Let's go eat," suggested Hrór.

After a huge breakfast, which Uncle Stoppard loved because it involved gallons of hot coffee, we headed over to the highway. Teemu and Gisli the Viking were remounting the tires. Brand-new tires. Once the last lug nut was screwed into place, we re-bungee-corded our gear back on the roof of the bus. The wind blew harder today. Gray clouds gathered in the west. We covered the luggage with a flapping square of yellow tarp, in case of rain. Hrór said goodbye to his family, hugging them by the side of the road. The tall grass behind them made a sighing sound.

Uncle Stoppard climbed onto the bus ahead of me when I spied, far below the farm valley, a shadow on the asphalt ribbon. Another van. The Viking family spied it, too. Not a lot of traffic in this part of Iceland. This highway led only to the Thorsfell. People who used this road either lived around here or were mountain climbers. As I watched the tiny van grow larger, I kept wondering, Ackerberg or Ice Flo?

"No, no!" shouted Teemu. Was he yelling about the strange van?

Edo, still standing by Hrór's family, yelled back at his brother in Icelandic. Teemu jumped out of the driver's seat, banged out of the minibus, stomped around the back, and threw open the hood. Or whatever they call it. With his flashing eyes and black goatee, he really looked like a demon now. Edo joined him and the two brothers stared at each other, amazed. Words thundered between them. They were either complaining or reciting one of those long epic poems Uncle Stoppard had mentioned yesterday.

"I don't have a good feeling about this," said Kate.

The motor was wrecked. The rat, the same rat who had slashed our tires, had yanked out the electric wires for the battery.

"I don't believe this," said Roobick.

"I knew we should have walked," I said to Uncle Stoppard. We would never see Tquuli or Thor's Belly Button. Why were the Ackerbergs doing this? Or the ice-cube spies? Whoever it was, why didn't they simply blow up the van? Or burn down the barn?

"Why didn't you two boys check the wires before?" demanded Roobick.

Edo threw up his hands. "We did not think this would happen."

"Why is this happening?" Teemu said angrily to Roobick. "Who wants to keep you from climbing the Thorsfell?"

The Jokkipunkis were thinking the same thing I was.

Edo's velvety eyebrows shot up his forehead. "The Curse," he said.

Not again. I closed my eyes, I didn't want to hear it. There is no curse. Please take away the curse.

HONK!

A purple van pulled up next to the minibus. Painted on its side curled a winking black cat wearing a crown. Mrs. Hrór frowned at the cat, pulling the two smaller Hrórs against her skirt. The driver of the van rolled down the window and stuck her head out. "Need any help?" she boomed. She was a large woman with cheeks as round and red as two Wisconsin apples.

"Wow, purple nuns," I said.

"Not purple nuns," said Edo.

"Okay, lavender."

"They are not nuns," he said.

"Nurses?"

"It is Asatru."

At first I thought Edo was saying the name of a Japanese or European van. Asatru, it turns out, is the name for the ancient religion of Iceland. It means "truth of the gods." The seven ladies in purple robes who rode the van worshiped goddesses like Freya, who drives around the sky in a chariot pulled by cats.

The Thorsfell, according to the van's driver Jorun Grettasdottir, should be renamed the Freijafell, in honor of the mighty goddess. Seems Thor bullied her off the mountaintop. Anyway, Jorun and her friends were on their way to the ancient volcano for some kind of midnight ceremony and were more than happy to give us a lift to our base camp. I didn't care how we got there—scooter, skateboard, or dogsled—as long as we got there.

"See? Things have a way of working out," said one of the nuns as we motored along the lonely two-lane road in the colorful van. Stranger things have happened, I thought. Roswell. The Bermuda Triangle. The election of a bald, former pro wrestler to governor of Minnesota. And the nuns' purple robes were a lucky color, like my Vikings sweatshirt.

The Zwake-Roobick expedition was crammed into the back two seats; the ladies sat in front. Our mountain of luggage was roped onto the roof. The nuns had helped us toss and bungee it up there with the skill of rodeo riders. They would make a great volleyball team.

I turned in my seat and glanced behind me. A hungry expression ruled Mr. Roobick's face. His mouth twitched, he could almost taste that ice. I felt like that, too. My toes tingled. My feet were itching to stand on the same rocks, the same lava flow, that my parents had stood on. Hrór's sneaker prints on the wooden beam back at the barn had given me an idea about my parents' interrupted footprints in the snow. I could hardly wait to reach the Thorsnafli and test a theory I had.

A nun pulled a guitar out of a case. "Shall we sing?" she said cheerily.

Hrór leaned over the front seat.

Women in purple
Freya's faithful followers
Share their chariot.

The nuns all went gaga over Hrór. Edo rolled his eyes under his bushy brows. Teemu shifted in his seat, conveniently settling closer to Sarah O'Hara. I consulted my journal, then craned my neck to look past the crowd of bouncing purple headdresses in front of me.

Off in the distance Fujiyama of the North lay waiting for us.

6
Deadmen

Base camp was a one-room wooden cabin no bigger than our living room back in Minneapolis. One door, two windows, a small electric heater, a clean, empty floor, and a single electric bulb in the ceiling. After the nuns, uh, Asatru sisters, parked their purple chariot, they joined us for a few hours. We shared an early dinner of cheese, tiny cakes, nuts, oranges, bananas, and dried fish smeared with thick butter. Bedtime came early; the floor was wall-to-wall sleeping bags. I used to think Uncle Stoppard's snoring was bad. *Uff da!* That night in the warm, crowded cabin, it sounded as if thundering Thor and Freya (including all her cats) had joined us. The nuns got up around midnight and tiptoed out. I waved to Jorun from my sleeping bag, then fell back to sleep.

Edo and Teemu shook us awake while it was still dark out. I hurriedly slipped on my climbing boots and cap, and ran out the door. Then I walked over to Edo, who was lighting the camp stove for breakfast, and asked, "Um, where do I go for . . .?"

Edo laughed. "Anywhere you want," he said.

I was glad the nuns had driven off to a different side of the mountain. Sarah O'Hara and Kate Roobick were still inside the little cabin, so I ran to the other side of the cabin, away from the door, and took care of business. Walking back to join the others, I glanced up the monster slope of the Thorsfell. There were no rest rooms on the way up there. So what did we do?

I found out once we started climbing.

Thor's Mountain is a gigantic pyramid of ancient lava and ice. Smooth slopes angle up to a snowy, craggy crown. From a distance, as we approached in the purple van, the white snowy slopes looked like paper. The lava slopes below resembled smooth black leather. Under a magnifying glass, paper and leather reveal little bumps and cracks and creases. So did the Thorsfell, the closer we got. When we started climbing, the creases and ridges increased.

"There are two kinds of lava," Edo told us. "Block lava and smooth lava. Block lava is hard and rough and can chew up your boot soles. Smooth lava is easier to cross."

"And more dangerous," Teemu said.

Smooth lava is lava that has cooled faster. Which means the cooling rock may have trapped a gas pocket or air tunnel beneath its surface. Under an innocent-looking field of smooth stone may lurk a dangerous pit. A crevasse! That's one reason we climbed roped together.

Teemu and Edo had a small, hushed argument about the division of climbing teams (I think it had something to do with Sarah O'Hara). Eventually we were divided into four sets of climbing partners: Teemu and Sarah, Mr. and Mrs. Roobick, me and Hrór, then Edo and Uncle Stoppard. Green nylon ropes, about fifty or sixty feet long, were strung between partners. The ropes were attached with sturdy metal clips at each end to our high-tech climbing harnesses.

The first method of climbing was simply walking. We grabbed our walking axes and headed slowly up the slope, all together. Partners remained separated by fifteen to twenty feet. In case one partner crashed through the lava, the other partner could help anchor the sliding rope—if he was quick. The lava beneath our boots was the color of dried mud mixed with tar. It was unnerving to know that while in some places the lava was as solid as concrete, in other places that lava was only a few inches thick, forming the thin roof of a cavernous gas bubble waiting to collapse and swallow us whole. Sometimes we walked across the back of an elephant, sometimes the skin of a balloon. Whistling breezes rustled tufts of emerald grass sticking through the cracked elephant skin. An occasional eagle would scream out of nowhere, then vanish. Sweat ran down my back, but the climb itself was not difficult.

"This first slope is graded F," Hrór told me.

"Mountains get graded?" I said.

"*Ja,* and F means *facile.*"

That stands for "easy" in French, the international climber's language. The first time getting an F is a good thing.

"Hey, Hrór, where do we, um, go for . . .?"

"Anywhere you want," he said. He sounded like his cousin.

"Yeah, but what about . . . you know, the other?"

"Don't worry. I have brought American toilet paper," he said.

"What are you boys laughing about?" asked Uncle Stoppard.

"Nothing."

By the middle of the morning the slope grew steeper.

"This must be forty degrees," I heard someone say. People's voices sounded different out here on the quiet mountain. The only sounds were the wind, the blood pumping in my ears, and the scrape of our boots on the rock.

"Forty degrees?" I said. "It feels warmer than that."

"Forty degrees," Hrór said, climbing parallel to me, fifteen feet away. He tilted his hand at a sharp angle, parallel with the slope. Wow, it really was getting steep.

The view was amazing. Even with my sun goggles, the light was almost blinding as it reflected off the snow and ice surrounding me. I was looking down the slope of the world's greatest snowboarding chute. At the bottom of the chute sat a tiny white cube, our base camp cabin.

We halted to catch our breaths. I leaned on my walking ax. Sarah and Uncle Stoppard rested on their knees, facing up toward the summit. As the angle of the mountain went up, so did the grade. Now it was PD, *peu difficile,* sorta difficult. White snow was replacing the dark, brown rock.

The second method of climbing would be popular with the Zwake family: It called for deadmen. Climbers who had traveled this route before us, including my parents and the trackers who had followed them, left metal anchors behind, pounded into the ground. These anchors were either *pitons* or *deadmen.* Pitons looked like tent stakes. Deadmen were shaped like flat, metal shovel heads. Both types of anchors had holes or rings for attaching our lines.

Climbing by deadmen was slow but safe. We climbed single file. Hrór and I were third in line to climb, Edo and Uncle Stoppard right behind us.

"Wait until I wave at you," said Hrór.

"Gotcha," I replied.

First Hrór climbed up about twenty feet and clipped his line to a deadman in the rock. Then he climbed another twenty feet to a second deadman. After he was attached to the second deadman, he waved. I angled into the mountainside, using my walking ax for extra leverage. It was warm, so I slipped off my nylon jacket and tied it around my waist. The sweat felt cool on my back. I still had on a thermal T-shirt and my purple Vikings sweatshirt (for good luck).

When I reached the first deadman, I unhooked the metal clip that Hrór had attached and stowed it in a pocket of my backpack. By that time, Hrór had already climbed up to the next deadman. This routine always kept at least two anchors between us in case we fell. *Glissade*, Kate Roobick called it. *Glissade* was a fancy way of saying slipping down the mountain on your butt. If conditions were right, and since the Thorsfell was a relatively smooth mountain, you could glissade all the way down to the little white cube. Maybe even to the Hrór family barn.

A new noise had joined the wind and the crunching of my boots. The jangling of Hrór's metal clips in my backpack.

I knew from Dad's notes that the Thorsfell was not a major-league mountain to climb. Intimidating, because of the height and steepness, but not impossible for beginner climbers. Not a stratovolcano, like the Oraefajokull to the south of us. After all, Ogar

Blueaxe and his buddies had dragged a Viking ship up here. And in those days they might have had deadmen, but they didn't have pitons or nylon ropes or plastic water bottles.

"Hrór," I called up to him. "I have a question."

"*Ja?*"

"If the Thorsfell has a low mountain-climbing grade, why don't more climbers scale it?"

"Well—"

That's when I crashed through the lava.

7
Hanging

A fist of pure ice knuckled into my belly button, seized my stomach, and yanked it out through the top of my head. The icy fingers froze my hair. A second fist punched me in the gut. Breath burst out of my mouth in a great sob, emptying both lungs in a nanosecond. The towline jerked at my harness. My neck cracked. My mouth opened, but no words came out. I couldn't feel my fingers.

A rough monkey paw brushed against my face in the darkness. No, it was the towline. I was hanging upright in the darkness. My towline stretched from the clip on my harness, an inch above my navel, to a spot somewhere above my head. My face bumped against the green nylon rope. I gripped it with both hands.

No wonder it was so dark, I still wore my sun goggles. I pulled them off over my glasses and let them hang around my neck.

Below me someone was smashing plates and glasses against a marble floor. Above me came a voice.

"Finn! Can you hear me!"

"Uncle Stoppard, is that you?"

A confusion of other voices, then Uncle Stoppard's again. "We're going to get you out of there," he said.

Where was I?

I had a memory of seeing the snowy landscape tilt past me. A rush of cold, stale air. A hollow feeling in my toes that rapidly engulfed me like a pool of ice water.

"Where am I?" I said. My voice echoed all around me in the darkness.

I was in a gas bubble. Trapped in one of those pockets beneath the smooth lava that Edo warned me about. My neck was stiff, but I glanced upward. A dark sky of stone pierced by a bright blue hole. My green towline traveled upward and hung from the edge of the blue hole. I had no way of judging how far away that hole was. A shadow blotted out the light.

"Finn! Can you see me?" It was Uncle Stoppard's face. I'd know those aquiline nostrils anywhere.

"Get me outta here!"

"We're working on it, buddy. Hang on."

Hang on? I still gripped the towline. I cautiously peered toward my feet. They dangled in space; a black nothingness hung below them. The dishes and glasses I heard smashing on a marble floor must have been the rocks I crashed through. The rocks that had formed the space where the sky-blue hole blazed overhead.

More voices trickled down through the hole.

"No, we can't pull him up. Look at the rope."

"What is that stuff?"

"Obsidian, and it's as sharp as glass."

I had seen a piece of obsidian in my geology class. The teacher passed it around and let us each touch it, a sharp, smooth shell of black glassy rock. Obsidian was formed by volcanic heat and pressure. Since the Thorsfell was a volcano, there must be miles of the stuff around. Maybe that's what I broke through, a layer of obsidian.

"Keep holding, Hrór!" someone yelled.

"Don't move that rope. It's like pulling it across a razor."

Razor?

"I've done this before."

"You're crazy!"

"Got any better ideas?"

"We don't know how big the roof is."

"We could be sitting on it right now."

"Okay, stake that line down, then unclip Hrór. We all need to move—"

The voices faded. Pebbles from the blue hole rained down on my cap. Another shadow blotted out the light. Uncle Stoppard again. "We're sending down another line, Finn. Think you can grab it?"

"I don't see it."

"We haven't tossed it down yet. Hold on."

The gas bubble was freezing. The air must have been sitting in there for a million years, never touched by the sun's warmth. Was I breathing in pre-historic bacteria? Microscopic dust from a woolly mammoth's hide?

"Here ya go, buddy." A nylon rope uncoiled past me, straightening itself like a thin blue worm. I gripped it with my right hand.

"I've got it," I called out.

"There should be a clip at the end," called Uncle Stoppard. "Fasten it to your harness."

I drew up the length of rope and found the metal

clip. It hooked easily to the center of my harness. "Okay, I did it," I said.

"Fastened?"

"Yup."

Loud voices. "Watch it, it's slipping!"

"No, that one! The other one!"

I heard a scream.

"Grab it!"

I dropped into space. My lungs filled with cold air. The harness jerked a second time; the new rope had grabbed it. A long green worm, the first rope, fell past me in a graceful tangle. Seconds earlier I had been hanging from that rope. I watched it disappear into the blackness below my floating boots.

The transfer of my weight to the new rope swung me back and forth over the pit, dangling like the spiders I'd seen in our living room. The spiders swung only a few centimeters in either direction. I was swinging by two or three yards, my body twisting and circling. Miles below me lay the rocky floor of the gas bubble. I listened for the sound of the first rope hitting the bottom, but heard nothing. Rope isn't very noisy, though, right?

"Watch! Watch it!" I think that was Edo.

My swing was now a few feet, back and forth. The blue hole above me seemed larger. It was probably my imagination; my eyes were adjusting to the dim light.

"Should I try climbing up?" I yelled.

"No! Just hold on." That was Sarah.

"Wait a minute, Finn," said Uncle Stoppard.

A dark head popped into view. Sarah was examining the rocky ceiling. She reminded me of a gopher sticking her head out of a hole, except that this gopher and hole were both upside-down. Sarah gripped a flashlight in her hand, playing its beam across the undersurface of the lava. I couldn't see what she was looking at. After a few minutes she pivoted her face to look at me. "Hang in there, Finn," she said. Does everybody have to say that! What else am I going to do?

Voices rumbled above me.

A third rope was tossed through the hole. "Clip that on, too!" yelled out Uncle Stoppard.

Why not? The more the merrier.

Another rumble above my head. This time it wasn't voices.

"Look out!"

Rocks pelted my head and shoulders. The blue hole tore open. I swung backward on the blue line. The new rope, though it was clipped to my harness, had a lot of slack in it. Maybe it hadn't been belayed yet at the other end.

The extra light pouring in through the widened hole gave me a better view of the gas bubble. The floor was still lost in darkness, but the walls appeared to be only thirty feet apart. The bubble was a round kettle, or cauldron. My boots had crashed through the thinnest section of the kettle's roof. Starting at the hole, the underside of the roof sloped downward and outward, thickening as it reached the walls.

Sarah popped her head over the edge of the jagged hole.

"Just a few more minutes," she said.

"That's what you said last time," I said.

"Who's keeping track of time when we're having this much fun?" she asked.

"It's cold in here."

"You'll warm up once you get out here," said Sarah.

If I get out there.

"Got that new rope attached?" she asked.

"Yup."

"Okay, we're going to pull you. Hold on." She popped out of sight.

The new rope straightened out, grew tighter. I felt it tug at my harness. The other rope, the blue worm, slackened.

The sky grew brighter as I approached the lip of the hole. Not again! More rocks rained against my head. The hole opened farther, like the lens of a camera. The new rope swung me forward against the wall of the gas bubble. I smashed into the wall with my gloves and boots, splayed out in an X shape against the rock.

"Finn, are you all right?"

"No."

The rock was freezing. I felt cold to the bone. And I tasted blood.

"We're still pulling," called Uncle Stoppard.

As the rope tugged me upward, I climbed against the wall. Knobs and ridges formed footholds and toeholds leading to the top of the kettle. I reached toward the hole's edge, gripping it with both hands. The rope tightened and yanked at the harness.

White light stung my eyes. Snow mixed with the taste of blood. Many hands grabbed my body and hauled me across the slope.

"Uncle Stoppard?"

"Yeah, I'm right here. You did great, Finn!"

"Excellent," said Sarah. "You knew just how to climb that wall."

"He cut his lip," said Hrór.

"You should come with us on our next ice-cube expedition," said Kate."We can use a climber like you."

"See any ice when you were in there, young man?" asked Roobick.

I shook my head. "Not unless it was black," I said.

I rolled over on my stomach, my thighs and back on fire. "This harness hurts," I moaned.

"We'll need to adjust it," said Edo. "It does look loose around the thighs. It might have traveled up your body a little too high."

"That can be dangerous," said Sarah.

"But it did its job," Teemu said.

Uncle Stoppard patted his glove against my back. "How are you feeling, Finn?"

"Like I just got the world's worst wedgie," I said.

Edo translated the technical term for his cousins. Hrór laughed so hard he got hiccups.

8
Clicking

"You bring us good luck, Finn," said Teemu.

"Because of my Vikings sweatshirt?" I asked, through swollen lips.

"You gave us our disaster for the climb," he said. "Most climbs have only one disaster, so now we are good for the rest of the trip."

"Like lightning never strikes twice, eh?" said Roobick.

After I had climbed out of the gas bubble, we made the unanimous decision to break for lunch. We sat in a group on the warm rock, all eight of us belayed, or secured, to three neighboring pitons. Cheese and chocolate had never tasted so heavenly to me before. As a treat, Uncle Stoppard produced a can of real American pop for the two of us to share. It had been hiding in his backpack.

"So where was the obsidian?" I asked.

Uncle Stoppard fizzed the pop all over his lap. "Er, forgot about the low air pressure," he said. "Obsidian? It was everywhere."

"The lip of the hole was obsidian," said Sarah. "Your towline, the first one, had already started to fray against the edge."

"Obsidian is like—*hic*—broken glass," said Hrór.

"That's why we threw down those extra lines," said Uncle Stoppard.

"And that's why I looked around that rock," said Sarah. "I wanted to see where the obsidian ended and gave way to another kind of rock. Luckily, the rest of the brittle obsidian broke off."

"When you get back to America," said Teemu, "I will give you money to buy me a lucky sweatshirt like that."

"You like the Vikings?"

"He likes the—*hic*—real Vikings," said Hrór.

"Maybe we will even see some real Vikings during this climb," said Teemu. "If you and your uncle find Tquuli."

"We'll find it," I said. Edo smiled at me beneath his velvety eyebrows.

"Kate and I are thinking of starting a Viking product line," Roobick tossed in. "So many great names for ice-cube flavors. Dragon this, blade that."

"Sword, spear, berserker," added Kate.

How about the ever-popular *ax?*

"The Vikings were not just warriors. They were also great poets and storytellers," Teemu pointed out. "And traders and merchants. Their colonies created the nation of Russia."

"America, too," said Edo.

"The Vikings may have added America to their old maps," said Roobick. "But the Indians were there first. And let's not forget the real discoverers of America."

"Who's that?" I said.

"The pioneers and cowboys," said Roobick. "You know, I like that name Tquuli. A good, exotic, mouth-filling sound. What do you think of Too Cool Tquuli?"

Teemu obviously didn't think much of it since he didn't make any answer. The disgusted look on Sarah's face matched the one on Uncle Stoppard's.

Kate wiped biscuit crumbs from her mustache, then clapped her gloves clean, her signal that lunch had come to an end. "What do we do when we reach the ice, gentlemen?"

Teemu produced a contraption from his backpack that looked like an oversized zipper. "We Jumar up the rest of the way," he replied.

Jumar is the brand name for a type of ascender. Like we say Kleenex when we mean tissues. Our ropes slipped through a hole at the top of the big zippers, and then it was simply a matter of clicking our way up. Clicking was easier than climbing the steep snow for those of us who were not experienced climbers. Uncle Stoppard, for example. He should have spent less time at that juice bar back at the Mall of America, and more time on the climbing wall.

"You up to climbing?" asked Sarah.

"I'm up," I said.

Before the Jumars, or ascenders, would work, someone had to climb up the slope first and anchor our ropes. Edo and Teemu were the frontmen. They swiftly clambered up the slope, swinging their axes and finding toeholds in the blinding white snow. Each of them pounded a new deadman in place, and threw down two lines. We took turns clicking up the ropes. The Roobick trio used one line, while Uncle Stoppard, Hrór, and I used the other. When we reached the new deadmen, we'd belay there and wait for the Jokkipunkis to climb up farther and set up the next deadman.

Sit, wait, climb, breathe. Sit, wait, climb, breathe.

Breathe in through your nostrils; the nose hairs warm the air before it gets to your lungs.

Climbers sniff a lot.

Besides the eight humans, we hauled up two big sacks of equipment with us. They held our sleeping hammocks, tents, cooking stove, extra lines, extra food, deadmen, pitons, and archeological and medical supplies. Between Roobick's Cubes and Uncle Stoppard's Ruby Raven money, a lot of dead presidents went into this expedition.

That's what Uncle Stoppard calls money. Dead presidents. Look at whose pictures are on the bills, and you'll see why. Dead stuff always follows me around, probably because I'm a Zwake. But this trip is going to be different. I'm going to find some live stuff this time.

Sharp, wintry wind blew down the sides of the Thorsfell. I had lotion slathered all over my face to protect from windburn, sunburn, and snowburn. Edo and Teemu wore little white sock-things over their noses. Teemu's goatee glittered with a thin layer of frost.

We had been climbing for two hours.

. . . click . . . click . . .

In a few more minutes we were going to make camp.

"Eeeeeuuuuuwwh!" I said.

"Quiet, Finn," said Uncle Stoppard in a loud whisper from the slope below. "No yelling up here, remember?"

Yeah, I forgot. On the snowy slabs and ridges of the Thorsfell we had to watch out for avalanches. Small noises can echo and ricochet like an invisible snowball, launching a dangerous wave of snow and ice.

"Sorry," I whispered back. "I couldn't help it."

I really couldn't. Because at that moment I got an answer to the question I had asked Edo this morning while he was lighting the breakfast stove. Down along the snow, trickling past my face and feet, hissed a yellow stream.

"Thanks for letting me try the American pop," called down Hrór.

"Yeah, sure, anytime."

The sun was still up when we stopped to bivouac. We needed to make camp while it was light out, while we still had energy. Uncle Stoppard and I used our axes to chip at the snow and ice, carving a small, horizontal ledge in the slope. He shot a look down the monster incline of the mountain and said, "This will be a new angle on sleeping." When I asked Uncle Stoppard if I could sleep on the *up* side, closest to the summit, he said, "Sure, Finn. If that's your inclination." He kept making corny puns like that while we pieced together the metal tubes that formed our pup tent, wrapped them in the nylon tarp, and shoved our sleeping bags inside.

"How's this taste, young man?" said Ruben Roobick, crunching across the snow toward our tent. He handed me a sliver of pure, cold crystal. I cautiously stuck out my tongue and licked. Hmmm.

"Cinnamon," I said.

"Excellent," said Roobick, nodding. "That's what I thought, too. Here, try this one." He handed me another.

"You'll spoil his appetite," said Kate, busy chipping away at her own sleeping ledge. I wondered if she had kids.

"What do you think?" Roobick asked me.

"Guacamole-ish," I said. Emphasis on the *ish*.

"Aahh," said Ruben. "I'll remember that one for the fast-food tacos."

Everyone was busy building camp, except for Mr. Roobick. He was scrambling around the campsite, straining as far as his belaying line would allow, chipping off a small ice chunk here, breaking off an icicle there. Then he'd scurry back, before it melted in his glove, and hand the ice to me or Hrór for tasting purposes.

"Yech," said Hrór, spitting out a sample. "Rotten cheese."

I licked another one that tasted like fried onions. Frozen fried onions.

Kate glared at her husband with Viking daggers in her eyes as she single-handedly erected their tent for the night.

Amazing! I never knew that ice could taste so different. And ice that hung or lay only feet apart from each other, inches in some cases. I asked the Ice Cube King what made the flavors.

"Many factors make up a single taste sensation," said Roobick. "The quality of the original lake- or seawater that evaporated, creating rain and snow, then ice crystals; or the subatomic organisms . . ."

"You mean . . . bugs?" I asked.

"Tiny, single-celled creatures," said Roobick. "They're everywhere. On our skin. In our drinking water."

"We can actually taste them?" I said.

"If there are enough of them," he said. "There's one little organism, I forget the name, that makes ice taste like vanilla ice cream. But if there are too many of the little buggers per cubic inch, then the ice tastes like cheeseburgers. What's that organism called, sweetie?"

Kate had crawled into her tent and didn't hear him. Or was ignoring him.

Dinner was cooked in a special aluminum-and-steel canister. We had sheep stew, sent along in plastic baggies from the Hrór farm. We also had our regulation cheese, chocolate, and Fig Newtons.

"I hope we packed enough food," I said to Uncle Stoppard.

"Plenty," he said. "Besides, humans can go up to three weeks without food."

Kate nodded over her steaming bowl of stew. "The Law of Three," she said. "A person will die if he goes longer than three minutes without air, three days without water, or three weeks without food."

There was an ocean of water around us, frozen into place. Food I wasn't so sure about. Not the way Uncle Stoppard likes to snack. I was also not too sure about sleeping on the side of a mountain, hundreds of feet above level ground.

Before we went to bed, Hrór treated us to another haiku.

Climbing the Thorsfell
Like bugs on a monster's back;
The ice dragon sleeps.

All the grown-ups clapped.

Hmmm. I cleared my throat and started, "A bunch of the boys were whooping it up in the Malamute Saloon—"

"That's enough whooping," said Uncle Stoppard, dragging me toward our tent.

Once I crawled inside the pup tent and snuggled into my sleeping bag, it was like being inside a tent anywhere. In a few minutes our bodies' natural heat began filling the nylon cocoon. Only my face stuck out of my sleeping bag. While I spoke to Uncle Stoppard, I watched my breath make smaller and smaller vapor clouds until they vanished.

"Everyone makes such a big deal over those stupid poems," I said. No one seemed to remember that a few hours ago I had been hanging for my life inside a prehistoric gas bubble.

"Hrór was pretty worried about you today."

"Yeah?"

"Both he and Sarah volunteered to climb down after you."

"Wow! I thought Sarah was just Kate's assistant. How does she know so much about climbing?"

"She's a research assistant. She doesn't just sit behind a desk. She accompanies Kate on her ice-cube expeditions."

"How were they going to climb after me?"

"On separate ropes. We were nervous about the obsidian cutting through your line. It looked pretty bad, Finn."

"Really?"

"Really."

Uncle Stoppard clicked off the flashlight.

"Lightning never strikes twice, right?" I said.

"That's what they say," he said.

Hmmmm.

"Good night, Finn."

I stared at the nylon roof above me, rippling in the wind. My muscles ached across my thighs where my harness had held me suspended above the gas bubble floor. My swollen lips throbbed in time with my heartbeat. Silence gripped the side of the Thorsfell. Uncle Stoppard must have been exhausted; he wasn't snoring. What if he rolls over in his sleep and pulls the tent along with him? Wrapped in nylon and metal tubes, we'll go glissading down the Thorsfell, Indiana Jones style. I'd had enough falling for one day. Wait, our tent was belayed. We were sleeping in our harnesses, also belayed to pitons and deadmen. I felt for my safety helmet and set it next to my pillow so I could grab it in the dark.

9
Goblin Wall

Snow.

We weren't expecting it, but the next day we ran into a lot of the white stuff as we clicked up the slopes. It sparkled like thousands of soft, tiny diamonds, whisking past our goggles. Like fake glitter you buy at a party store. As Minnesotans we should have been used to it, but it made me dizzy. Uncle Stoppard called it "disorienting." As I clicked my way up the slope, the snow fell past me at a faster rate than I was moving upward. My confused brain thought I was moving in slow motion. A few times I misjudged my footing, or moved too quickly, and slipped down the slope a few feet.

The snow stopped after an hour. It started again after lunch.

In the early afternoon we reached the foot of an intimidating cliff.

"I thought it was a smooth slope all the way up," I said.

"Up to this point," said Teemu. The cliff was a hundred fifty feet high. The Goblin Wall, they called it. Sometimes the Glittering Wall, *Glitraveggur*.

"Why Goblin Wall?" I asked Hrór.

"The *huldufolk*," he said in hushed tones. "The

hidden folk. The goblin servants of Thor live in cliffs just like this one."

"So, it's like climbing over their house?" I couldn't believe I was asking Hrór these questions. As if I really believed in these creatures.

"Nothing will happen," said Hrór.

"That's good." I didn't want Hrór to think I was making fun of him.

"The goblins only come out at night," he said.

Edo pointed to the icy ledge above us. "That's Thorsnafli," he said. "Just over that edge."

Thor's Belly Button was so close!

"Now we take a vote," Teemu said. "It is still daylight. Do we climb the Goblin Wall and camp at Thorsnafli tonight? Or do we rest and bivvy here, and climb first thing in the morning?"

"We climb," I said.

"That's one vote," said Edo.

I elbowed Uncle Stoppard.

"Uh, yes, I say we climb," he said.

"Two for climbing," said Edo.

"Should be two and a half," I whispered to Uncle Stoppard. "You're the tallest person here."

It was unanimous: climb. "With the Jumars and crampons, we should reach the nafli while it is still light," said Teemu. Crampons were metal shoes that clamped onto our boots. Eight sharp spikes stuck out from the shoes in all directions. As we clicked upward along the face of the cliff, we were to dig our feet into the ice. It kept us from twisting in circles on the ends of our lines. It also helped us climb faster and took some pressure off the ascenders.

As before, Edo and Teemu went first. They halted twenty feet above our heads and hammered in the pitons. This time we all climbed together. On our line Hrór went first, then me, then Uncle Stoppard. Roughly twelve feet of rope separated us from each other.

It was the hardest work I've ever done in my life. Even though the ascenders did most of the climbing for us, I used every muscle I had to push upward, stay steady, and keep myself from banging into the rock and ice inches from my nose. Now I know why climbers wear helmets. The occasional grunt from Uncle Stoppard, climbing below me, was a good advertisement for them. Mr. Roobick, clicking up his line fifteen feet to my right, slipped a few times. His aquiline nose collided with the icy wall.

"How does it taste, honey?" his wife called up to him once, teasing him. I noticed she wasn't having that easy of a time, either. Sarah O'Hara looked sure and graceful as she eased up the rope. She reminded me of Batgirl scaling the side of a building, creeping up on the unsuspecting bad guys hiding on the roof. She had the same determined chin, the same unblinking eyes.

"What's that?" she yelled.

Sarah disappeared. So did Roobick and his wife. A white cloud surrounded us. A *hot* white cloud.

"Hang on!" I heard Edo shouting from up above.

Was the volcano erupting?

Everyone dug in with their crampons and held the lines. The clicking of the ascenders stopped. A rushing hiss of steam echoed around us.

"I think it's a steam vent," I heard Uncle Stoppard say, hanging below me, invisible in the thick white cloud.

"It is a steam vent," Edo called down. "Minor volcanic activity. All of you stay where you are."

"The goblins must be angry," joked Roobick.

"It will stop after a few minutes," said Teemu.

He was wrong. More steam hissed from nearby hidden fissures in the cliff wall.

"Yup, it's ten minutes again," said Kate, timing the steam with her watch. I was surrounded by a wall of white mist, goblin breath. Scraping sounds came from above. I heard hammers pounding into the ice.

"What's going on?" I asked.

I looked up and saw a boot descending toward me.

"Our plans have changed," said Edo, swinging into view. "Can you all hear me? We are camping here tonight."

"Here?" came Roobick's voice.

"We'll use the hammocks and sleep here tonight," Edo said. "No problem. It is better if we don't move until we can all see clearly. And the steam makes the ice slippery."

"How long will that take?" asked Kate.

"I can't believe this will last more than a few more hours," said Edo. "But it will be dark by then. Do not worry. Teemu and I will take care of setting up the hammocks."

Teemu scraped into view alongside his brother.

"We'll need to haul up the equipment sacks," he said to Edo. "And we need to bring the two lines closer in together."

Great! It started snowing again. I wondered if the goblins could control the weather.

The snow did one good thing. It dissolved the volcanic steam enough so that we could all see each other again. Our world had dwindled to the size of Hrór's barn. The world had only eight people in it, a ton of rope and equipment, and a slice of icy mountain. Nothing else was visible.

It was cool to watch the Jokkipunkis set up our bivvy, or bivouac, while hanging in space. The ringing of their axes mixed with the hissing of the steam. I closed my eyes at one point and pretended I was in the belly of a huge, old-fashioned steamship like the *Titanic*. The brothers belayed hammocks to the wall with dozens of pitons.

Mountaineering hammocks are different from the common lawn hammocks that hang from a metal frame, or sag between two trees. These resemble cots without feet, stiff metal frames with tightly stretched nylon beds. Some climbers call them portable ledges. Five hammocks soon jutted out from the side of the Thorsfell: mine and Uncle Stoppard's, the Roobicks', Sarah's, Edo's, and one for Teemu and Hrór. The equipment sacks dangled below. Our campsite resembled a bunch of window washers suspended on the side of a wide, windowless skyscraper.

The hammocks were wide enough to support a tent. Once we each climbed onto our individual floating porches, the nylon beds springy as mini-trampolines, we carefully pieced together our tent poles and clamped them into place. During this whole time, each of us was also belayed to the side of the cliff. The Goblin Wall was a high-tech spiderweb humming with colorful human bugs.

"You sure those pitons will hold all night?" asked Uncle Stoppard.

"Special pitons," said Teemu. "We call them Viking Claws."

Cool name.

Edo chuckled. "You will not be falling down like Jack and Jill," he said. "We have done this before."

Didn't he and Teemu say they had climbed the

Thorsfell five times? Then why didn't they remember the Goblin Wall and the steam vents? Why hadn't they taken us up a different route?

"Is there another way to get to Thor's Belly Button?" I asked.

With the falling snow, the steam, and the gathering darkness, it was impossible to see each other well enough as we talked. Instead, we all yelled out into the air while we sat on our hammocks, eating from the food we carried in our individual backpacks. We could hear the different voices coming from different directions around us.

Teemu's voice did not sound amused. He was tired from the extra, unexpected work of setting up a hanging camp. He also sounded as if he knew why I was asking my question. Did he think I lacked respect for their skills?

"This is the easiest and quickest way," said Teemu flatly. "Unless you come by helicopter."

"There is another route," said Edo, below us. "But it would add at least three days to our climbing schedule."

"Let's hope this minor volcanic activity doesn't add three more days," Kate added, off to our left.

"Does she sound a little steamed to you?" Uncle Stoppard asked me, grinning.

At least it would be warmer while we slept. The volcanic mist warmed the surrounding air. It no longer felt like winter, but early fall. Water droplets gathered on all the shiny metal parts of the camp. I removed my gloves and nylon jacket before I climbed into the sleeping bag.

The inside of the tent felt different tonight. The nylon floor gave slightly when I crouched on my hands and knees.

"It's a hammock, Finn," said Uncle Stoppard. "We won't fall."

"Promise?"

"You're belayed to the side of the cliff. Even if the hammock fell, you wouldn't."

"I'm sleeping with my helmet on."

I wanted to ask Uncle Stop what he thought about mythical goblins crawling out of the rocks at night. *Huldufolk.* I decided against it, I didn't want him to think Hrór actually believed in that stuff.

A bright blue sky greeted us the next morning. The goblin steam had vanished completely.

So had Edo.

10
Body Bag

"Impossible!" cried Teemu.

"I don't believe it," said Sarah.

"Goblins," said Hrór.

Edo's tent was Edo-less. His entrance flap was unzipped, waving like a flag in the morning breeze. His harness, still belayed to the side of the mountain, lay empty on his sleeping bag.

"Has he fallen?" asked Kate from her hammock, hanging a few feet away from me and Uncle Stoppard. I had thought the same thing. But if he had fallen, wouldn't his harness be outside the tent, banging against the side of the cliff? Grabbing a set of binoculars from my backpack, I scanned the base of the Goblin Wall. A hundred feet below me, the new-fallen snow lay in a wide, white patch, undisturbed and printless. No body, no footprints.

"I don't see anything," I said.

Kate held on to a belay line and stretched out her other hand toward me, across the gulf between our hammocks. "Let me see those, young man," she demanded.

I carefully handed her the binocs, then turned to Uncle Stoppard. "When did it stop snowing?" I asked. "Did it snow last night?"

"It snowed while Edo and Teemu hammered our campsite together," he said.

"That didn't last long."

"Fifteen minutes," he said. "Then there was a clear sky. A full moon. Not completely dark out."

"How do you know that?"

"I woke up in the middle of the night," said Uncle Stoppard. "Thought I heard something, a scraping sound, and was worried about those pitons coming loose."

"The Viking Claws?"

"Yes, and when I unzipped the tent and looked around, the steam had dissipated by then. The sky was perfectly clear."

"And there was a full moon?"

"Yes, a hunter's moon."

Hmm, were the goblins out hunting last night?

The snow below us was fresh. If Edo had fallen, or for some weird reason climbed down in the middle of the night, he would have left footprints. How could he have climbed down without one? And why would he have attempted such a dangerous feat, especially considering what had happened to me earlier in the day?

"Hrór, check that other sack," Teemu directed his cousin.

"The sack?" said Hrór.

"Do what I say!" Teemu was ticked.

The two equipment sacks, side by side, hung six or seven feet directly below Edo's hammock. The left sack, where we had stuffed our hammocks and tents, now hung like a limp balloon next to its bulging twin. Hrór scrambled down from his hammock, still strapped into his harness, belayed like the rest of us to the side of the Goblin Wall. His digging crampons made short, quick rasps as he quickly descended. While the Haiku King neared the equipment sacks, Teemu held Hrór's belay line taut. The rest of us held our breaths. What did Teemu hope to find in the full equipment sack?

If the icy *Glitraveggur,* the Goblin Wall, were the face of a massive clock, Uncle Stoppard and I were hanging slightly beneath the center of the clock face. Our hammock, I mean. The rest of the hammocks spread in a rough semicircle around us. Edo was at five o'clock, the lowest point of the campsite, the Roobicks at nine o'clock, Sarah at four o'clock, and Teemu and Hrór at two o'clock.

Hrór searched through the equipment sack. He turned his puzzled face back up toward his cousin. "What am I looking for?" he yelled.

"Edo!" said Teemu. "Maybe he is pulling a joke on us."

Some joke. Poor Hrór shook his head. "No . . . just supplies."

At four o'clock Sarah scanned the snowfield below us through her own set of neon-pink binocs. She sat back on her haunches and stared up toward the edge of the cliff.

"Anything?" asked Uncle Stoppard.

She shook her head. "I don't understand it," she said, looking down at us from her hammock ledge, her green eyes full of fear. "Where did he go?"

Goblins?

Edo's harness was abandoned. No prints disturbed the smooth snow below us. No pitons were hammered into the cliff face above us. It was as if he had flown away. My stomach suddenly turned into a Roobick's ice cube. Edo's disappearance . . . my parents' disappearance. "As if the Zwakes had been lifted up into the air." The friendly Jokkipunki with the velvety eyebrows had suffered the same mysterious fate.

"We must go down," said Teemu. "We must leave this place."

"We can't!" Did I say that out loud?

"We cannot climb without Edo's help," said Teemu. "And we must tell the authorities, the police. We must begin a search."

"I can help," said Hrór. "Climbing, I mean. You know my parents were trackers."

Teemu shot Hrór a warning look. "Yes, your parents," he said. "But not you. We need help. A search crew."

"Radio for help," said Uncle Stoppard.

"Ja, vist!" exclaimed Teemu. He ducked into his tent for his two-way set.

I looked at Uncle Stoppard. "Why did you have to say that?"

"What do you mean?" asked Uncle Stoppard.

"We can't stop now!" I cried. "We're so close."

"This is an emergency," he said.

"So is getting to the Thorsnafli. Offer him more money."

"What?"

"Give Teemu more money. Give him a thousand more dollars if he'll take us up to Thor's Belly Button."

"Finn—"

"People like money. Mr. Roobick said the Jokkipunkis would do anything for a buck, right?"

"You need to calm down, Finn. Edo's disappearance is an emergency situation. He could be hurt, lying somewhere."

"Don't you get it? He disappeared," I said. "Just like my parents."

Teemu crawled out of his tent, his face pale. His voice shook slightly. "I cannot raise anyone on the radio," he said.

"Try it again," said Sarah.

Roobick's voice boomed behind me. He was standing on his hammock, peering over ours, and facing toward Teemu's perch at two o'clock. "I'll add a thousand dollars a day, if you'll continue the climb," he said.

"See?" I said to Uncle Stoppard. His cucumber eyes grew squinty.

"I cannot," said Teemu.

"Two thousand," called Roobick. "Take us up to the Thorsnafli and then back down tomorrow."

"But the search—" Teemu stared.

"We're your search team," said Roobick. "We may not be professional trackers, but we are first on the scene. Who's to say your brother didn't climb up the cliff last night?"

"There are no Claws in the cliff," said Sarah O'Hara.

"None we can *see,*" Roobick pointed out.

"This is ridiculous," Kate said.

"Why would Edo climb up the cliff?" asked Teemu.

Roobick shrugged. "You yourself thought he might be playing a practical joke." Roobick pointed a gloved finger toward the foot of the cliff. "There are no signs he went down. He must have gone up."

"What if he didn't?" said Sarah in a quavery voice.

Roobick laughed. The first comforting sound that

morning. "You think he flew away like a bird?" he said.

Hrór, meanwhile, was rummaging through Edo's tent. Kate was the first one to notice something odd that morning. She had pointed to Edo's tent. We all saw the entrance flap rippling like a flag, but no one had actually gone into the pup tent before Hrór. I assumed Kate and Roobick, from their vantage point at nine o'clock, could see right into the empty tent at five o'clock. The hammock I shared with Uncle Stoppard was positioned high enough to not be in their line of vision. Edo's tent was the lowest cocoon in our spiderweb of nylon and aluminum. Had something crawled up from *below* and unzipped his tent?

Hrór stuck his head back out the opening. He looked up at Teemu and sadly shook his head. Teemu was busy fiddling with the dials on his compact radio. Static sputtered out of the device.

"What do you say, Teemu?" asked Roobick.

"Uncle Stoppard, why don't you offer more money, too?"

"Finn, please!"

The remaining Jokkipunki stroked his goatee. "Two thousand, you said?"

"It will take another rescue team at least twenty-four hours to get here," Roobick said. "If and when you contact someone. We could be on our way back down by then."

"I can help with the Claws," said Hrór.

"We need to hurry before those steam vents start spouting again," said Kate. "I don't want to hang around another long day doing nothing."

Me, neither.

"What do you say, Teemu?" asked Roobick.

"Just a moment." Teemu put the radio's head-phones back on his head and spoke a few words in Icelandic.

"He's got someone," said Hrór.

"Drat!"

"Finn!"

"Did I say that out loud?"

After a short, frantic conversation into the radio, Teemu spoke to the rest of us. "A rescue team will leave this afternoon," he said. "But it will take more than a day to get here."

"Just as I said," said Roobick.

"What about helicopters?" asked Sarah.

Teemu shook his head. "Not on this side of the Thorsfell," he said. "The downdrafts are too danger-ous."

"My offer still stands, Teemu," said Roobick. "It makes no difference to the rescue team if they reach us at the top or the bottom of this wall."

"Well—"

"And if we reach the Thorsnafli, we may have found out what happened to your brother."

"Maybe he found another way up," I said.

Teemu stoked his black goatee. "Hrór, get back up here."

"Why, Teemu?"

"You have to help me place the Claws after break-fast."

"Hurray!" Did I say that out loud, too?

Breakfast was more like instant breakfast, choco-late and cheese in thirty seconds. Hrór and Teemu climbed up the remaining fifty feet to the ledge of the cliff, securing pitons and belay lines. We strapped on our crampons for more click-and-climb. The first secured lines that Teemu and Hrór threw down to us were clipped to our hammocks, tents, and supplies. Then we humans hung from the cliff wall while still attached to our individual belay lines. We released our sleeping ledges from their former belay ropes and watched them swing out from the ice wall. Two more lines were tossed our way, and our ascenders were fastened to them. This way, once the entire Zwake-Roobick team (minus one) had reached the Thorsnafli via ascender, we could haul our gear up after us on the other, free-hanging ropes. It was faster than taking apart all the tents and hammocks and restuffing them into the empty equipment sack. Time was pressing on us. If Edo was in trouble at the top of the cliff, we needed to reach him as swiftly as possible.

. . . click . . . click . . .

Uncle Stoppard kept mumbling to himself as we ascended the remainder of the Goblin Wall. I heard the words "dead air" several times. Dead air? Where had I heard that phrase before?

When I finally reached the lip of the cliff, Teemu and Hrór grasped me under my armpits and lifted me to my feet. Uncle Stoppard and Kate were the last to appear over the icy edge.

Have you ever gotten one of those fancy, pop-up birthday cards? The kind you open up sideways, and a colorful, cut-out scene pops into place? Thor's Belly Button was like one of those cards, but magnified three hundred times. We stood on a wide, snowy ledge (the bottom half of the birthday card) which faced a wide, smooth cliff (the upper half of the card) the same size as the ledge. The ledge and cliff were both the length and width of a football field. At our backs was the top of the Goblin Wall, and below that the slanted slopes which led down to the foot of the Thorsfell.

The upper half of the Thorsnafli was magnificent. Massive and white, as smooth as an outdoor movie screen. The lower half of the Thorsnafli, the ledge section we stood on, was the parking lot for the drive-in theater. The movie screen/cliff wall was a rough circle, enclosed by jutting ridges of stone above it and framing it on either side. Viewed from a distance, I could imagine how Viking warriors (and merchants and traders) would have believed the white, gleaming circle in the middle of the volcano was a belly button. A real big belly button. The snow even looked like lint.

"Gorgeous," said Sarah O'Hara.

"I can almost taste it," said Roobick, licking his lips.

While everyone else was hypnotized by the view, Uncle Stoppard tapped me on the shoulder. I followed him as he jogged back toward the supply ropes.

"Help me pull these, Finn," he said.

"What, now? We can't do it alone," I said.

"Never mind. Just start pulling."

"But what's the—? "

"I want to check out that other supply bag," he said grimly, tugging on the line.

"You think something is missing? Besides Edo, I mean?"

"I think there's a body inside."

11
Staring at Thor's Navel

"A dead body?" I said.

Uncle Stoppard adjusted his gloves on the line for a better grip. "A living, Finnish, pit-bull body," he said in a low voice. "Shhh. Don't say anything." The others were walking over to join us.

Edo hiding in the equipment sack? It was the only logical, nongoblin explanation possible. That's why Uncle Stoppard was mumbling about dead air. *Dead Air* was the name of that new mystery he was working on. The one with the dead body stuffed into a carry-on bag in an airplane. Uncle Stop figured Edo was hiding and playing a joke on us. Some joke. I didn't think Ruben or Kate Roobick would laugh.

All six of us had grabbed on to the supply ropes like teams playing tug-of-war. A few minutes later, one of the hammocks rose into sight, and rolled over the edge followed by the equipment sack. Uncle Stoppard grabbed on to the sack and pulled it farther up onto the ledge.

"I'll just get this out of the way," he said. Hrór gave us a funny look.

Uncle Stop and I dragged the sack along the snow. While the others were tugging up the rest of the tents and hammocks, I nervously unzipped the long blue nylon sack. Coils of nylon rope, clips of pitons, a first-aid kit, flashlights, shovels, packets of dried food. More archeological tools rested in a small case at the foot of the bag. Everything was there except a joking Jokkipunki.

Uncle Stoppard frowned. "Hmm, no Finn in the bag."

"What did you say?" asked Teemu. He stood behind us.

"Uh, no, Finn," said Uncle Stoppard. "In the bag . . . um, is where we'll keep the flashlight. Oh, hey, Teemu, didn't see you there. Sorry. Are you guys already finished with the other gear? Thanks. We, uh, we were looking for something."

"Did you find it?" Teemu asked. The cold air had frosted his goatee again.

"Yes, yes, thank you," said Uncle Stoppard. "But we'll, uh, leave it in the bag for now."

"In the bag," I said.

We crunched across the snow toward the Thorsnafli. "Does this mean you're going to rewrite *Dead Air?*" I asked.

"Shhh!"

"And if you thought Edo was in the bag, why didn't Hrór see him?"

"Maybe Hrór was in on the joke."

"Hrór wouldn't do that," I said. "Not for just a joke"

"How about for extra cash?" said Uncle Stoppard. "The slashed tires bought the Jokkipunkis another day's worth of guiding. You saw how Roobick offered more money to climb up here."

"Two thousand more."

"Extra money for the same amount of work," said Uncle Stoppard.

That's just what Ruben Roobick had said the first day we met him at the airport. But for some reason, I still couldn't see Hrór lying like that.

"So where's Edo?" I said.

"There has to be a rational reason—"

"A hang glider!" I cried.

"What?"

"In the middle of the night Edo assembled a portable hang glider," I said. "There was a full moon, right? You saw it."

"And Edo flew down the Thorsfell?"

"You don't think that's possible?"

"Possible, yes, but not likely," said Uncle Stoppard. "For one thing, it's dangerous. Mountains create unpredictable updrafts and downdrafts. Why would Edo glide down the mountain?"

"He's working for the Ackerberg Institute," I said. "It is their mission to prevent us from coming to Iceland and discovering my parents."

"Finn, do you know what the word *paranoia* means?"

"It means you think that people are following you."

"And . . .?"

"What? We're being followed?" I grabbed my binoculars from my backpack and ran to the lip of the cliff. Nope, no signs of people anywhere on the slopes. I wondered whatever happened to those purple nuns.

"Finnegan," said Uncle Stoppard. "I think you worry too much about the Ackerberg people."

"Finn, Stoppard! Over here!" Sarah waved us over to the Belly Button. "I want to take a picture of all of us," she said. Sarah crunched her backpack down in the snow, then balanced an automatic camera on top of it. She set the timer and trotted over to join our group, snuggling close to Teemu. We herded together with our backs to the movie screen of the Thorsnafli. The camera beeps grew louder and faster.

"Everyone smile!" she cried.

"Cheese!" said all the Americans.

CLICK!

The air grew dangerously still. "Is that thunder?" I asked. Out of the corner of my ear, I heard a faint rumble. Teemu whipped around and stared up at the jagged ridges of the Thorsnafli and the snow slabs beyond. The ground shook gently beneath our boots.

"Avalanche," whispered Hrór.

Great. First obsidian, then goblins, now a mountain of snow.

The rumble faded away. Everyone let out a breath.

"We must be careful here," said Teemu. "Avalanches are common during the summer. There is snow backed up on those ridges." He nodded toward the upper reaches of the Belly Button.

"Sorry about that," said Sarah. She retrieved her camera and backpack.

The two Roobicks went strolling off toward the left, or west side, of the Thorsnafli, ice-flavor hunting. Teemu reminded us that when the search-and-rescue team arrived during the next two days, we would have to obey their decision. They might decide it was for our own good to vacate the mountain and come back another time. Until that decision was made, Mr. Roobick wanted to taste as much ice as he could. Teemu and Hrór wandered off to the east side of the ledge, searching for signs of Edo.

I felt utterly helpless. "We can't do anything in one day," I said to Uncle Stoppard.

"Let's do what we can," he said. "We can always come back up."

"Really?"

"We'll mount another expedition."

"Our own private, personal expedition."

The first thing I wanted to do was examine the snow ledge, check out the spot where my parents had camped. Consulting my journal, and the article and photos from the *Peephole* article, I found a spot where I thought my parents' footprints had been discovered. In the background of the old black-and-white pics stood a funny banana-shaped rock. If I found that rock, and stood in the one spot where the rock matched the angle of the picture, I should be standing near the footprints, right?

Eight years led to this point. An empty field of snow. What had I expected? That my mother would be standing here, would rush to my side, her long black hair falling loose from her cap, and then crush me against her parka in the best bear hug in the world? Dad would jump up from his camp stool, not caring that he dropped his pen and journal on the snow, and run over to join us. Then I would hear a word, one word, one single syllable. A word I dreamed of hearing for eight years. My name said aloud in my parents' vanished voices. That's all. Then we would stand there forever. I didn't care what happened after that.

Nothing would ever come between the three of us again. Nothing.

Nothing was there but an empty field of snow.

Maybe there was a reason, a purpose I was left behind in Minneapolis. "See? Things have a way of working out," said one of the purple nuns as they drove us to the mountain. I was left in America so that eight years later I could come back here and solve this mystery. No one else cared enough to solve it except me. And Uncle Stoppard, of course. The trackers they brought in to search for my parents didn't do such a hot job. They didn't even find clues. Only those footprints that ended abruptly in a field of clean, smooth snow.

Hrór's footprints back at the barn had given me an idea. Those sneaker prints had also ended abruptly, but I knew the reason behind that particular mystery. Hrór had simply stepped off the beam. I wondered if my parents had done something similar. What if they had jumped from the field onto a nearby rock or boulder?

I glanced around. The banana rock! It stuck out of the snow along a ridge of rock at the eastern edge of the Belly Button. I held up the photo to get my bearings. A few more feet to the left, several more feet back. This was it! I was standing in the same spot as the footprints, at almost the exact center of the ledge.

The ground was smooth. Undisturbed, lintlike snow covered the level field. There was no way my parents could have jumped twenty or thirty yards to the nearest rock. Even Spiderman isn't that good.

Then I had another idea. Hrór had fallen down. *Down!* The trackers and reporters thought my parents disappeared by going up. *Lifted into the air.* No one thought about looking in the opposite direction. People were so concerned about not disturbing the footprints, the only remaining evidence, that they didn't think to look *under* the snow. I was the only one to think of it because they were my parents. Part of my purpose, my reason.

I snatched my walking ax from my backpack. The snow and ice at my feet flew out in shiny, jagged chips. Nothing but lava. Well, there was lots of snow to look under.

The sun was setting behind the western ridge of the Thorsnafli. Long purple shadows fingered their way toward me across the snowy field. The small figures of Teemu, Kate, and Sarah were setting up camp behind me, blinking on a miniature lantern in the dusk. Must be nice to have all the time in the world. I didn't! I needed to find something, anything, under that silent, evil, stupid layer of snow.

A figure I was expecting crunched his way toward me. "Finn, it's getting late."

"I don't feel tired at all."

"We need our energy for climbing back down tomorrow," Uncle Stoppard said.

"Since we're coming back up here anyway, I've decided to stay."

"Stay? Oops!"

A chunk of ice flew out from beneath my ax and hit Uncle Stoppard in the chest.

"Wear your goggles," I said.

"Finn, don't you think—?"

CLANG!

I stopped chipping, breathless. "That was metal," I said.

Uncle Stoppard stared at me. "Yes, it was," he said slowly. "Metal, not snow."

He pulled out his own walking ax and joined me. The ice and snow flew from beneath our axes as if it were being attacked by twin snow-blowers. The field between the ridges grew deep purple.

"Look at it!" I cried.

"I don't believe it," said Uncle Stoppard.

At the center of our minor excavation, a rough circle in the ice and snow, lay an ancient iron ring, as big as a doughnut. The doughnut was attached to a door.

12
Ogar's Secret

"What's the rush?" asked Ruben Roobick.

People are so nosy. Uncle Stoppard and I had run back to the equipment sack to fetch our flashlights. I don't know why Uncle Stop had to tell them, but I guess they'd find out soon enough.

"Oh, nothing," I said.

"Finn solved the mystery," said Uncle Stoppard.

"Thanks a lot," I muttered under my breath.

"What mystery is that?" asked Kate Roobick.

"The Zwake footprints?" said Sarah.

"His parents?" said Kate.

Hrór jumped up from his campstool. "Parents!" he cried.

I don't know why he was so excited. Teemu got a weird glint in his eyes and said, "Ogar."

"An ogre?" asked Roobick, confused.

"Ogar Redaxe," explained Teemu. "The first Viking to climb the Thorsfell."

"But not the only Viking," added Uncle Stoppard. "He and his shipmates supposedly dragged a Viking ship all the way up the side of the mountain."

Did he have to tell them the whole story? Let them read a book or surf the Web like we did. Now everyone would know about the Viking treasure and the Haunted City of Tquuli.

"The ship was most likely not one of the traditional longships," said Sarah. "They were, what, eighty or ninety feet long? I'd say Ogar's vessel was probably a *knorr,* a smaller merchant ship."

"The gold was Italian, not Viking, right?" asked Kate.

"I thought the Viking's name was Skuld something-or-other," said Roobick.

Great. The entire expedition party was familiar with the legend. Too familiar. When Uncle Stoppard blabbed about the metal door, the rest of the Zwake-Roobick expedition (minus one) jumped up, threw away whatever they were eating, grabbed flashlights from the supply sack, and jogged over to the field behind us. I do not like crowds. A million flashlights were aimed at the metal doughnut as Teemu and Uncle Stoppard tugged it open.

Sloping downward from the thick, metal door ran a smooth, round tunnel.

"A volcanic vent," said Sarah.

"A door to *Bilskimir,*" said Hrór, in a spooky voice.

"What's that?" I said.

"The fortress of Thor," Hrór said. "It has five hundred and forty doors."

"Drafty," I said. Maybe Thor liked having lots of visitors. Or maybe Freya did, if the purple nuns were right. How could a modern-day normal teenager like Hrór believe in things like Thor and giants and goblins? If I lived in a country where people vanished off the sides of cliffs, maybe I'd believe in weird stuff, too.

As soon as I ducked below the metal door and set

my feet on the smooth, rocky floor, I couldn't see my breath anymore. "It's warm in here," I said. Must be thermal activity beneath the rocks, like the Witch's Cauldron and the steam vents in the cliff. I pulled off my knit cap and unzipped my nylon jacket.

I was at the head of the crowd, along with Uncle Stoppard. The glare from the other flashlights shone like daylight at my back.

"Hold your flashlight steady, Uncle Stoppard."

"I can't, I'm too excited."

"What's that?" I said. My beam picked out something glittering on the floor of the tunnel.

Uncle Stoppard stooped over and picked it up.

"Gold," said Teemu.

"Mmmm, not gold," said Uncle Stoppard. He held it up before my eyes. A small, hollow, brass-colored cylinder.

"A shell casing from a bullet," said Roobick.

Sarah bent in closer for a look. "A lipstick cover," she said.

Lipstick?

"I haven't seen a metal one in years," said Sarah.

Uncle Stoppard handed me the lipstick cover and I shoved it in a jacket pocket. It might be only brass, but it was gold to me. It was proof we were on the right trail. Thor doesn't need lipstick and neither does Freya. Why would a goddess (or a goblin) need lipstick? Humans do. Human, female, American archeologists.

"How would Ogar get a ship down here?" asked Teemu, somewhere behind me. "The door's too small, and the tunnel is too narrow."

"There must be another entrance," said Sarah.

One of those other five hundred and forty doors.

"Oh!" yelled Uncle Stoppard.

"What is it?" I asked.

"Um, I hit my head on the ceiling," he said.

"The Vikings were considerably shorter than their modern-day descendants," said Sarah. "I think five feet eight was the average."

Edo and Teemu were the right height for Vikings.

"Uncle Stoppard," I whispered.

"Yes?"

"Is Teemu carrying his ice ax?" I said.

"I don't think so. Why?"

"Just curious." Ogar's blue ax turned red inside this mountain, perhaps in this same tunnel we were exploring. I wonder what his buddy Skuld's last name was. Bonesplitter? Skullcrusher? Redaxe Two?

The lipstick cover was the only thing I saw that was out of the ordinary. A modern invention in an ancient tunnel. Otherwise it was just rock and more rock. No signs reading THIS WAY TO TQUULI. I glanced briefly behind me, watching the other expedition members. I couldn't distinguish faces. They were moving shadows, backlit by the glare of the flashlights, one behind the other.

Roobick was talking the entire time to his wife and Sarah. "This would make a great commercial," he said. "A long traveling shot through the tunnel. Winding, twisting. Spooky electronic music. Maybe some rap. Then a bright light up ahead. And, exploding onto the screen, the new Viking flavors!"

"Berserker blueberry," said Kate.

"We could fly a film crew up here," said Roobick. "Show the actual tunnel that we discovered. That'll give customers a real thrill."

The tunnel that *we* discovered?

"Sarah," said Kate. "Are you remembering all this? We need to write it down when we get back to camp."

"Forget about camp," said Roobick. "I'm staying in here tonight."

I must have slowed down, because Uncle Stoppard was now a few steps ahead of me. His boots scraped over the rocky floor.

"I found something!" yelled Hrór. We gathered around him, our beams spotlighting his freckled face and glasses. His ungloved hand held a black, frozen scorpion.

"Yuck, what's that?" asked Uncle Stoppard.

"A crampon," said Teemu.

"Oh."

The spikes of the crampons did look like stubby scorpion legs. The dangling bootstrap was even curled into a poisonous, tail-like shape.

The crampon must belong to the original Zwake climbing party. If the trackers had found it, they would have taken it with them. What am I saying? The trackers never got this far. Hrór turned to his older cousin and breathed, "This proves they were here."

I heard Sarah's whisper to Kate magnified in the round tunnel. "Their names were Anna and Leon, short for Leonardo."

"Ah, yes," said Kate.

"Does Leonardo Lemon have too many syllables?" asked Roobick.

My mom and dad had discovered this tunnel eight years ago and climbed inside. When they slammed the doughnut door shut behind them, the snow and ice frozen to the outside of the door must have blended in with the snow nearby. Like one of those secret doors that trapdoor spiders make to conceal their underground nests. That's why the footprints looked as if they ended in the middle of nowhere. The crampon and the lipstick cover proved they were in here. But why leave a crampon behind? Did they not plan to climb back down the cliff? Perhaps, as Sarah suggested, there was another way out, a secret back entrance that only my parents had discovered.

We continued along the warm tunnel. I was half expecting Hrór to make up one of his weird haikus. Yup. Behind me I heard,

Into the tunnel
Visitors to Thor's fortress,
Looking for secrets.

That wasn't so bad, I guess. Let's see. I counted syllables on my fingers.

Lipstick and crampons
Were not made by the Vikings—

"Hey, there's a cave up here," called Uncle Stoppard. He stepped through the end of the tunnel and disappeared.

"Where'd he go?" said Hrór.

Uncle Stoppard had stepped down onto the floor of a vast, black cavern. At least, we thought it was vast. The walls were lost in darkness.

The mouth of the cave, where the tunnel ended, was as round and black as a dragon's throat. I took a step to follow when Uncle Stoppard appeared in my flashlight beam, flinging out his arm.

"Finn," he said. "Don't go in."

What was his problem? After days of climbing and trudging through the snow, eight years of wondering what happened to my parents, I was not going to turn around now. I pushed past Uncle Stoppard and then froze. Warm perspiration gathered on my forehead. I think I stopped breathing, but I still saw my breath in front of me. The cave was cold.

The light from the six flashlights at the mouth of the tunnel gleamed on something a few feet in front of me. Something white lay on the floor of the cave, but not as white as the snow outside.

Bones.

"Look!" cried Hrór. "Two skeletons!"

13
The Viking Claw

I saw the claw.

White, skeletal fingers groped over the top of a boulder. A spider of frozen bones. Two leg bones stuck out from behind the boulder's bottom edge. The claw and legs were connected to a full skeleton. A second skeleton lay two or three yards beyond the first, its arms flung out on either side of the hollow rib cage. The skull grinned up at the dark ceiling. A glimmer of gold caught my eye. On the wrist bone of the arm lying nearest me something glittered.

A wristwatch.

Back home in Minneapolis, I keep a photo on top of my dresser. It's the brightest spot in the apartment. It is also the only picture I have of my parents and me together. I'm sitting on my mom's lap, my dad next to us, a picnic blanket spread out around our knees. Snapped a month before I moved in with Uncle Stoppard, the pic shows the hot sun of Agualar beating down on us. All three of us are squinting into the camera. The sunlight gleams off a golden statue my parents dug up in Agualar called the Horizontal Man. Sunlight also gleams on my father's wristwatch.

I've stared at that photo so many times during the past eight years that I have memorized each detail.

The seashell print of my mother's dress. The palm-patterned shadow on the picnic blanket. The flexible metal band and the crystal of my father's wristwatch. The same watch that now encircled the bony wrist of the second skeleton.

"Stop it!"

The cave revolved like a washing machine. The smooth floor rushed up savagely, striking my cheek. Flashlights snapped off. A sudden rumble of thunder, then silence.

"Finn! Finn!" It was my uncle's voice, echoing down a long dark tunnel.

Something was wrong with the flashlights.

"Finn, wake up!" Uncle Stoppard said.

Two huge cucumber slices were hanging over my head. A waterfall of red flame. Uncle Stoppard's eyes, Sarah O'Hara's hair. They were kneeling next to me, studying my face.

"The flashlights," I mumbled. "They're wrong."

"Finn," said Uncle Stoppard.

I sat up. I had been lying on the cool floor of the cavern. "It's not the gas bubble again, is it?" I asked.

"Gas bubble?"

I turned my head. Skeletons. Oh, yes, that's what happened.

Uncle Stoppard began, "They may not be—"

"They may be Vikings," said Sarah. "Look at the ring."

Ring?

A thick gold ring circled one of the bony fingers. A dragon, carved from the gold, brandished wings and jaws. I didn't remember that in the photograph. Did my mother find that ring and slip it on her finger eight years ago?

"It's definitely not Italian," Sarah said. "Or American. I'd say northern European."

Hrór was bending over the skeletons. He looked as worried as I felt.

"How did that wristwatch get here?" I asked.

"I don't know, Finn. But I recognized it, too," said Uncle Stop.

"It can't be the same one."

"Lots of people buy that style watch," said Sarah.

"Yeah, lots," I said weakly. "Hrór?"

"Ja?"

"Is there any . . . writing on the watch?"

He tenderly slipped the watch off the wrist bones. The arm fell back with a dry clatter against the rock. Hrór flipped the watch over and sighed. "Letters," he said. "There are letters carved on the back side."

"Anything with a Z?" I asked.

"Ja, A.Z. to L. Z."

The cave floor started moving again.

"Oh, Finn." Sarah hid her face behind her long hair.

"But what about the helmets?" said Uncle Stoppard.

I slowly got to my feet and walked toward the bony claw. I glimpsed a pale gleam of a skull on the other side. Well, I came this far, I can't stop now. A crumbling leather helmet, decorated with bones, crowned the eerie skull. A tattered belt of leather and metal bits drooped across its pelvic bones. Near the second skeleton's right arm lay another helmet, dented and bronze-colored. Would my parents, in their excitement over discovering Tquuli, have tried the helmets on? I would have. Taken pictures, too. There weren't any cameras lying around.

Was this black cavern Tquuli? I shivered. The cavern's cooler air reminded me of the stale, cold atmosphere of the gas bubble. The cold must have helped preserve the leather helmet and belt. The rest of their clothes had deteriorated.

Wait. Plastic doesn't deteriorate. All of those people who talk about protecting the environment tell us that plastic pop bottles and CD wrappers will last for a thousand years. That's why we recycle it, instead of tossing it away.

"Uncle Stoppard, what is this I'm wearing?"

"Uh, clothes."

"I mean, what is it made of?"

"Mm, nylon, I guess."

So where are the nylon parkas and leggings and gloves my parents wore during their expedition? Stolen? Why would a thief steal modern clothes that can be purchased anywhere, yet leave behind two priceless Viking helmets?

I grabbed Hrór, standing nearby, and pulled the collar of his jacket down in the back. There was the label.

"What's going on?" said Hrór.

I saw the words: Shell & Lining, 100% Nylon. In the *Peephole* pics of the four Icelandic archeologists who worked on the Zwake team, they wore clothes similar to our own climbing gear.

"They're naked," I said.

"What?" said Uncle Stoppard.

"It's too cold in here to be naked."

Uncle Stoppard reached his hand to his head. Dried blood stained his forehead.

"What's that?" I asked.

"Nothing. Must be where I hit my head in the tunnel," he said. "Too bad I'm not as short as a Viking."

Yeah, like Edo and Teemu. Wait a minute! Short like Vikings.

"How tall are you, Uncle Stoppard? Six one, six two?"

"You feeling all right, Finn?"

"How tall are you?"

Uncle Stoppard turned to Sarah. "He thinks we're back on the plane."

"Was someone naked on the plane?" Sarah asked.

"My dad was tall, too, right?" I said.

"Yeah, as tall as I was. Am. I mean, he am. I mean, we're the same size."

"Do we have a tape measure in the supplies?" I asked.

"In the archeological supplies, yes."

I looked at the skeleton claw gripping the boulder. "I think ... I think I know how to prove those are, uh, those are someone else." One of Ogar's buddies, I prayed.

"Uncle Stop, could you please go get the tape?"

"I'll get it," said Sarah.

"What's your idea, Finn?" asked Uncle Stoppard.

I whispered to Hrór. "Do me a big favor. You know which tent is ours? At the bottom of my sleeping bag I stuffed a paperback. A book. Bring it here, but don't let anyone see it."

"You don't think the skeletons are your parents?"

"I don't think they're anyone's parents. I mean, not for the last thousand years anyway. Quick, go get the book. *Don't* let Uncle Stoppard see it!"

Hrór grinned at me and darted off.

Something red stained the white chin bone of the first skeleton. Blood?

"What's that?" I pointed.

"The mandible," said Uncle Stoppard.

"Not the chin," I said. "I mean, what's that red stuff?"

We both took a closer look. "Lipstick, I think," said Uncle Stop.

Lipstick that belonged to the brass cover I had found in the tunnel.

"It's a rune," said Uncle Stoppard. "Someone used red lipstick to mark a rune on the chin."

Dad's research journal for the trip to Iceland contained a section on runes. He had copied pages and pages from four or five library books. Runes were letters, part alphabet, part magic. Vikings used them for writing spells or stories.

"Where's my backpack?"

Uncle Stoppard had used it to prop up my head on the rocky cavern floor. He tossed it to me, and I pulled my journal from one of the zippered pockets. Dad's stuff was sandwiched between its pages. I riffled through the sheets and found the page that showed each rune and what American letter, or sound, the rune stood for. I examined the skeleton's chin again. I mean, mandible. Then I matched it with the right rune.

"It's an A," I said.

"The A sound," said Uncle Stoppard. "Like 'ah.' "

Why did she write that?

Sarah and Hrór returned a few minutes later. Where was the rest of the Zwake-Roobick expedition? Sniffing out various corners of the cavern. Their flashlight beams fluttered like white moths against the cave walls. Hmm, something about those flashlights.

Sarah handed me the tape.

"Do you know what your humerus means?" I asked Uncle Stoppard.

"It means you think I'm funny," he said.

"The humerus," I explained patiently, "is your arm bone. Upper arm. And the ratio of your humerus to your total body height is approximately 20 percent."

"How do you know that?" he asked.

"Uh, something I read."

Uncle Stoppard turned to Sarah again. "Probably from one of my forensic books back home," he said with a grin. Uncle Stop has tons of reference books on dead bodies and poisons and guns and stuff. That's not where I got the info about the humerus. It came from Mona's newest book, *Cold to the Bone.* Her super detective, an African-American named Revelation-of-St.-John Bugloop, half pygmy, half French, solves the puzzle of the reverse-microwave oven killer by examining the victims' bones. Mona put in real forensic details, just as Uncle Stop does in his books. Anyway, Mona explained that scientists can determine a person's height just by looking at their skeleton. Your body's largest bones, the humerus, the femur, and the tibia, always correspond to your height.

"The humerus," I continued, "is, uh, part of your total height." I turned around, took the paperback Hrór held hidden behind his back, and flipped through the pages.

"What are you looking at, Finn?"

"Just thinking." Ah, there was Mona's description. I tucked the book in my back pocket and turned around to face him. "The humerus," I continued, "is 20 percent of your total height. So, if my father was six feet two, I mean *is*—"

"Yes?"

"Then his humerus should be roughly . . . 20.72 inches."

"Good head for math," said Sarah.

Especially arithmetic and geometry, since they were invented by dead civilizations. See? The dead stuff again.

"Why not simply measure their heights?" asked Sarah.

"It's too inaccurate," I said. "Skin and muscles and cartilage and stuff add to your height, too. But that stuff is all dissolved." Looking down at the skeletons, I said, "Let's measure the humeruses."

"Humeri," corrected Sarah O'Hara.

"Yeah, and their femurs, too. Femurs are about 28 percent, and tibias come in at roughly 23 percent."

We tape-measured all three bones on both skeletons. Uncle Stoppard wrote the figures down in my journal. After a few moments of calculation, we made our discovery.

"Isn't that great, Finn?" said Uncle Stoppard.

"They're Vikings," said Sarah. "Smaller bone structure."

"They couldn't be Icelanders?" asked Hrór.

"Then where are their modern-day clothes?" I pointed out.

"They also had really bad teeth," said Sarah.

"My parents?"

"The Vikings."

"Uh-oh. The wristwatch," I said.

Uncle Stoppard nodded. "I know. That watch belongs to your dad, all right. But we can't figure out how, or why, it got on that fellow's wrist." The skeleton wearing it was three to four inches shorter than my dad.

My head was feeling better, the skeletons were not Zwakes. But then, where were my parents?

"This is cool," said Hrór, touching the dragon ring on the Viking claw.

Roobick, Kate, and Teemu were still examining other sections of the cave. The corner of my eyes kept catching their flashlights dancing along the rocky walls.

"Uncle Stop," I said. "How many flashlights are there?"

"Are you feeling all right?"

"Yes, I'm fine. How many?"

"Well, we each have one. That makes six. I mean, seven, counting yours."

When I first saw the Viking skeletons, I had glanced back at the mouth of the cave. Six flashlights burned in my eyes. Six flashlights aiming at the bones. But Uncle Stoppard had stepped aside. He was standing a few feet from me, not at the mouth of the cave. The two of us were already inside the cavern. That means there should have been only five flashlights at the mouth of the cave.

Who was holding the extra flashlight?

14
Popsicle

"This could be a clue," said Uncle Stoppard. He held out the wristwatch. Hrór had given it to him before fetching Mona's book from my tent.

The two hands were frozen at nine o'clock.

"What happened at nine o'clock?" I asked.

He shrugged. "Maybe it's the number nine he wants us to think about."

Sarah wriggled her nose. "Or it could be the shape of the clock hands. If you're looking for a clue, I mean. Instead of nine o'clock, maybe it's really a backward L."

"Or a frontward L if you look at it upside-down," I said.

"No," she said. "If someone had wanted to show an L, they would have set the watch hands to three o'clock."

"Assuming it *is* a clue," said Uncle Stoppard.

"It has to be!" I cried.

My voice echoed against the ceiling. Teemu jogged over to us. I quickly pocketed the wristwatch in my jacket and stood in front of the skeleton's red-stained chin.

"Feeling better?" he asked.

I nodded.

Uncle Stoppard explained our discovery about the skeletons.

"Well . . . that's good."

"Look what I found over by that wall." He held out a bright gold coin. A winged lion was etched on one side.

"Oh, Teemu," said Sarah, giving him a kiss. "It's Italian!"

"I, uh, um, also found a helmet, a belt buckle, and a gold armband. It's incredible," said Teemu. "These are national treasures!"

"That's terrific!" added Sarah.

"You think this is Tquuli?" I asked.

"What else could it be?"

"Yooowwww!"

"That was Ruben," said Sarah.

"Over here, quick!" yelled Kate.

They were standing next to a ridge of dark red rock, partially hidden by white mist.

"A steam vent," said Kate. "It burned Ruben's hand."

"It's nothing," he moaned.

"Let's look at that," said Teemu. Roobick's hand was bright red, as if he had dipped it in the Witch's Cauldron. White spots started puffing up. "It is already starting to blister," added Teemu. "Let's get some antibiotic."

I leaned over to Uncle Stoppard. "Can't we stay down here and look some more?"

"Look at your watch," he said. "It's getting late."

I forgot that outside the sun was setting.

Dinner was brief but exciting. Everyone chattered about the Viking discoveries in the cave. Except for Roobick, who sat glumly with his hand wrapped in a bandage. "I think it's a myth," he said.

"Tquuli?" asked Edo.

"Just a cave with a few trinkets."

"What about those skeletons?" I asked.

"A couple of poor souls who searched for the legend like we did," he said. "Only they realized sooner than we did that it *is* only a legend."

How can he say that? It was too soon to tell.

"If there was anything else in that cave we would have found it," he went on.

"It was a small cave, as caves go," agreed Kate.

"Tomorrow," said Roobick, "I'm staying above ground. Concentrating on ice."

Speaking of concentrating, I thought Sarah was concentrating a little too much on Teemu during dinner. Plus, he was making such moony eyes at her whenever she spoke. Yuck.

The next day it snowed. All day gentle flakes fell on Thorsnafli. True to his word, Ruben stayed outside and searched the rocky ridges for strains of exotic-tasting ice. Kate explored the tunnels with the rest of us.

"Ice is nice," she said. "But how often do you get the chance to make a discovery like this one, huh?"

I wished Ruben had joined us. Not because I missed him thrusting a chunk of ice in my face every five minutes, asking my expert opinion as a modern-day teenager, but because of the rescue team. I was hoping that we would all be underground when they arrived. They'd take one quick look around and go back to Reykjavik or wherever. With Roobick up there, they'd be sure to find us and haul us back to the city.

Uncle Stoppard and I brought up the rear as our party explored the tunnels. The dancing flashlight beams advanced before us. I wound my dad's wristwatch and strapped it on my wrist, slipping the brass prong through the highest punch hole. Too bad there wasn't a Mute button on the dial. Every noisy tick was another half-second closer to the end of the day. We must have tracked and retraced our steps through more than twenty miles of tunnels. We even stayed down there for lunch. No other caverns, and no sign of Ogar's treasure ship or a haunted city. Just a mess of dead ends. In a few of those dead ends, Hrór and I heard smooching sounds in the dark.

"My cousin is lovesick," he whispered to me.

Yuck.

"Why do you think none of these tunnels lead anywhere?" I asked.

"The Egyptians put fake tunnels in their pyramids to frustrate would-be grave robbers," said Uncle Stoppard. "Maybe the Vikings did the same thing."

"Or volcanic activity sealed up the tunnels over the years," suggested Kate.

"Goblins can seal up the ends of caves," said Hrór.

"Could Tquuli be fake?" I asked.

"Those two Vikings back there came from somewhere," said Uncle Stoppard. "Most legends have a basis in fact. Sarah said the coin Teemu found was Italian. That was part of the legend, too."

"We have to come back here!"

"Let's figure that out when we get to the hotel," said Uncle Stop.

A wristwatch and a lipstick. The only two pieces of evidence that my parents had been here. The crampon was also evidence, but it could have come from anyone. Another archeologist, a tracker. I suppose I should be glad that we didn't find any skeletons wearing nylon backpacks and climbing shoes.

No skeletons and no Popsicles.

Popsicle is a slang term used by police all over the globe when referring to a frozen dead body. I first saw it used in one of Mona Trafalgar-Squeer's books, *Murder on the Polar Express.* I saw my first Popsicle in Iceland, later that night.

We dragged ourselves up and through the doughnut door and wearily back to camp. I was freezing. The warm air in the tunnels confused my body temperature. You'd think that living in Minnesota would toughen my body for extreme climatic changes.

No one talked during supper. I never thought I'd get sick of chocolate. Everyone was thinking about the tunnels and about leaving tomorrow. Hrór looked worried; we had found no sign that Edo had climbed up the Goblin Wall.

Roobick handed me an ice chunk. "How's that?" he asked.

"Gloomy," I said.

Teemu avoided our eyes all through dinner. He felt people were blaming him, that it was his fault for wanting to return to civilization and gather a search-and-rescue team. Only Sarah would sit next to him.

"Still think we might have to leave tomorrow?" asked Roobick. He sounded pretty cheery for someone who had to leave.

Teemu shrugged. "It is up to the rescue team," he said.

Roobick turned to Kate. "What if we paid the rescue team a little extra, too?" Then he said, "What do you like better, Teemu? Teemu Truffle or Teemu Tangerine?"

"Or Teemu Treasure," suggested Kate.

As the sun edged toward the western side of the Thorsnafli, I walked near the *Glitraveggur* cliff. Scanning the darkening horizon and mountainside with my binocs, I saw no trace of Edo. No markings in the smooth slopes below us.

I was convinced that extra flashlight I saw back at the skeleton cave had been the other Jokkipunki brother. I still thought that Edo was playing a bizarre practical joke on us. Icelanders have a funny sense of humor. But if Edo was nearby, where was he? And how had he vanished from our hanging campsite on the Goblin Wall?

I liked believing that the extra flashlight had been in Edo's mitts. It was too spooky to think it belonged to someone, or something, else.

"Looking for Edo?" said Hrór. He had snuck up on me. I hoped he didn't notice that I jumped.

"Yeah, but there's nothing."

"It's a waste of time," said Hrór.

"Why do you say that?"

"It just is."

"What do you think happened to him? Think it was, like, goblins or something?"

Hrór laughed. "Goblins?" he said. "No, I do not think so."

"Then how?"

"Doesn't matter, does it?"

"It matters what you tell the trackers who come looking for him," I pointed out.

Hrór nodded sadly. "*Ja,* trackers," he said.

I took one more look down the mountain, before it became too dark. I saw a thin twig of smoke curling up off to the south. Hrór's farmhouse.

"Do you like living on a farm?" I asked.

Hrór stamped his feet to keep warm. "I'll get used to it."

"Didn't you grow up there?"

He looked at me with a weird expression. "I grew up north of here," he said. "Another city called . . . well, in English it would be called Midge Lake."

Midge. I knew that a midge was a small, annoying insect that flew around your head. Uncle Stoppard had mentioned that Iceland was free of mosquitoes, but he never said anything about midges. Midge was also the name of the hurricane that slammed into Agualar years ago, forcing my parents, and me, to leave the Mayan dig, chasing us away to Uncle Stoppard's apartment. Yeah, a midge can be annoying.

"In Icelandic we call it Myvatn," Hrór said.

"Sounds familiar," I said.

"It is pretty," he said. "Friendly. And a beautiful lake."

"Do you get used to them?"

"Used to who?" asked Hrór.

"The midges," I said.

"There are not so many. They fly over the lake. Food for the fish."

I turned my back to the cliff. The snow was covered with innumerable footprints from when we climbed over the edge, dragging our equipment behind us. Hrór's freckles stood out sharply against his pale, cold cheeks.

"It's too bad we're leaving so early," I said.

"Teemu says we have to," said Hrór.

"We just got here."

Hrór looked away. "We have to find Edo."

"Well, I hope you find him," I said. "I, uh, know what it's like to lose a relative."

"Parents," he said softly.

"Yeah."

I had an idea. "I'm keeping a journal of my trip," I said. "Everything that happened to me and Uncle Stoppard since we got here. And all about the climb and the Witch's Cauldron and sleeping in the barn and stuff. Well, would you mind autographing it?"

"Autograph . . . ?"

"Sign your name," I said. "I want to get everyone's name before we leave."

"Ja, okay."

Back at the campsite I handed a notebook around so that each person could write his or her name and address. I wanted to record all the details of our trip. In case Uncle Stoppard and I didn't return to Thorsfell right away, I wanted to review the trip on paper, hunt for clues. I told Hrór I'd send him a postcard from Minneapolis.

"The Mall of America?" he said.

Everyone knows about that stupid mall.

In our tent that night, huddling in my sleeping bag, I trained my light on the journal. I was reading names.

Ruben J. Roobick
Kathryn Roobick
Sarah O'Hara
Teemu Jokkipunki
Hrór Hrolfson

"Hrolfson? I thought he was Teemu's cousin?" I said.

"Cousins don't always share the same last name," said Uncle Stoppard. "In Iceland last names are complicated. For instance, Hrór's last name means he's the 'son of Hrolf.' But if he had a sister, say, Gertrude, her name would be Gertrude Hrolfsdottir."

" 'Cause she's Hrolf's daughter?"

"Right. See how complicated it gets? People in the same family have different last names. Hrór's dad has a different last name from Hrór, depending on what the grandfather's name was."

"So you could have the same last name, and not even be related to each other?"

"Uh-huh. That's why the phone books here in Iceland go by a person's first name instead of his last."

I flipped through the pages of my journal. For the thousandth time my eye landed on the *Peephole* article. I decided to skip it, but a word jumped out at me. Myvatn. That was where Hrór was born. The *Peephole* article said:

> Expert trackers from Reykjavik and Myvatn retraced Anna and Leon Zwake's route up the sloping side of Thor's Mountain.

I wondered if Hrór knew any of those trackers. Then I noticed the next sentence.

> Luckily, no rain or snow had fallen since the Americans had last radioed their friends from the famous volcano cone.

Radio.

"Have we heard any more from the rescue team on the radio?"

"I don't think so, Finn. I figured you were hoping that we didn't hear from them."

"Sort of." But there was something odd about the rescue team, just like there was something odd about that extra flashlight.

"Want to hear something odd?" said Uncle Stoppard.

Something else?

"I don't really believe it," he said. "But Roobick told me, and Teemu told him."

"Yeah?"

"Remember when Teemu first tried to get help? We were hanging on the Goblin Wall, and he ducked inside his tent after I suggested he use the radio."

"I remember that."

"Yes, well, when Teemu came back out of the tent, he looked all weird."

"Yeah, and he said he couldn't contact anyone."

"He did," said Uncle Stoppard. "But he heard something else on the radio that totally spooked him."

"What?"

Uncle Stoppard scrunched closer to me on his sleeping bag. "Edo's voice."

An ice cube dropped down my back.

"It was faint, but it was definitely Edo," said Uncle Stoppard. "At least, that's what he told Roobick today."

Voices.

"That might be why he's frightened about using the radio again," said Uncle Stoppard. "But we know the rescuers are on their way."

When I was standing by the cliff earlier, talking with Hrór, I had looked out over the mountain with my binoculars. No sign of Edo. No sign of an approaching search-and-rescue team, either. Were they climbing up a different route? Were they coming at all?

"Finn . . . are you still wearing your purple Vikings sweatshirt?"

"And my Vikings socks and my Vikings T-shirt."

"Ever since we arrived in Iceland?"

"Yeah, for good luck. Why?"

Uncle Stoppard sniffed. "A picture of our laundry room back home just flashed through my mind," he said. "That's all."

A picture of the two-way radio was flashing through mine. If Teemu was picking up Edo's voice, would he pick up other voices? Voices belonging to other people who had vanished?

As soon as Uncle Stoppard's welcome snores filled the tent, I zipped on my jacket, pulled my cap down over my ears, and tugged on my boots. My fingers were on the zipper to the front flap when I heard the crunch of boots. Someone walked past the tent. After about ten minutes, more crunching, growing louder, then fainter. Maybe Hrór was out sleepwalking. I thought Teemu had him tied into his sleeping bag. Quietly I unzipped the front flap and crawled out.

The moon was absent, but the sky still glowed bright purple from the setting sun. In summer, Iceland's sun sits just below the horizon at night. The eerie light made it easy to find my way over to Teemu's tent. Or was that Edo's tent? They were both neon green with black stripes. Edo's tent had not been dismantled once it had been hauled up over the cliff along with the others. Hrór was using it now.

I didn't see Hrór, or anyone else, crunching around the ledge. The campsite was silent. Snores rumbled softly through the air; otherwise it was as quiet as a Viking cemetery.

Teemu kept the radio on a small campstool beside his tent. The stool was missing. Great. He had it inside with him. If I unzipped the tent, it would wake him up. Maybe I should just go back to bed and try the radio in the morning. Would that be too late? What if the rescue team arrived before breakfast and I never got the chance to listen for those long-lost voices?

I gave a quick glance over my shoulder to make sure I was alone, then I softly approached the Jokkipunki tent. I hoped Teemu and Hrór were heavy sleepers, because it was one of them inside that tent. Whoever caught me, if they caught me, I didn't know how I'd exactly explain my actions. Sleepwalking like Hrór? I could say that it was contagious.

I hooked my ungloved finger through the plastic zipper ring. Removing my gloves, I figured, would give me a better grip when I slid the zipper open. I pulled up an inch. Nothing moved within the tent. I pulled another inch. Still quiet.

Feeling brave, I slid the zipper up two more inches. *Zzzhhip.*

Uh-oh. What if Sarah was in there with Teemu? And I caught them kissing or something. Too late now.

I saw the head. Teemu didn't wear a cap to bed. Didn't he get cold? What was I thinking? He lives in

Iceland, he's used to this climate. Hey, that wasn't Teemu, and Hrór's hair was red. This hair was light and wavy.

A dried, gaping wound sliced across Ruben Roobick's frozen forehead. He was as blue as one of his own ice cubes.

15
The Other Footprints

A Viking Claw stuck out of the Ice Cube King's chest. A dark patch, pooling outward from the deadly piton, stained his jacket. After seeing the twin skeletons down in the Viking cave, nothing could shock me anymore. Surprise me? Yes. Who would want Ruben Roobick dead? And what was he doing in the Jokkipunkis' tent?

I'm not going to tell anyone about the dead body, I decided.

At the side of the Popsicle formerly known as Ruben Roobick sat Teemu's two-way radio. If I woke people up now, I'd never get the chance to listen for voices.

I'll tell people in the morning, I decided.

After rezipping the tent, I hugged the radio to my chest and ran to the doughnut door. It was still hanging open from last night. Carefully I crawled into the tunnel, lifting the radio in after me.

Once inside, I pulled my flashlight from my jacket pocket. I was looking for a quiet place to turn on the radio. I figured someone might hear the hiss and crackle of the static if I stayed outside in the open air.

A few more steps down the tunnel, I scrunched

down against the wall. What was that on the floor? Blood. Not ancient, dried-up Viking blood, either. Recent blood. Blots and drips led down the tunnel.

I can't look at it, I told myself. I'll listen to the radio, crawl back into my sleeping bag, and let other people discover Roobick in the morning.

Drat! The radio didn't work. I switched on the power button, but there was no sound. The headphones were silent. Turning the knobs back and forth did nothing.

I looked at Dad's watch. Five o'clock. Uncle Stoppard and the rest would be getting up in an hour. Reluctantly I climbed back outside and returned to my tent. Good. Uncle Stoppard was still snoring. I shoved the radio sideways down into the foot of my sleeping bag, next to the journal and Mona's book. Tomorrow, when everyone was down searching the tunnels, I'd wait before I joined them. The radio might work better aboveground. Then, once I heard the voices, figured out where they were coming from, I'd return the radio to Teemu. At night. Anonymously.

Who would stab Roobick with a Viking Claw?

No, I won't think about it now. I can't. That's not my problem. Well, yes, it was. Once the rescue team arrived, they would definitely order us off the mountain. There would be a murder investigation, and who knows how long that would take? It might be weeks, *months*, before we could return to the Thorsnafli.

Why did the Ice Cube King have to die? It sure screwed up my life.

If I could figure out who killed him, and figure out what happened to Edo, then there would be no reason for an investigation. Uncle Stoppard and I could stay up here and search for Tquuli as long as we liked.

I must have fallen asleep, because the next thing I remember was hearing the scream. Uncle Stoppard dashed out into the morning light first. I checked to see if the radio was still in my sleeping bag, then joined him outside.

Sarah had screamed. Kate was staring, stone-faced, at her husband's frozen body. Hrór shouted and ran away from Edo's tent. He stopped about thirty feet away, his back to me and Uncle Stoppard, and shuddered in the cold morning light. Teemu's face was white.

"I don't understand," said Uncle Stoppard.

"I heard him get up in the middle of the night," said Kate. "I figured he was answering a call of nature. I must have dozed off. I don't remember him coming back inside."

"He must have gotten up early," said Sarah. "You know how obsessed he is with finding new ice flavors. And how he wanted to stay longer."

"That's not my fault," said Teemu. He stood very straight and still.

"No one says it is," said Uncle Stoppard.

"She will. She will say we were arguing yesterday," he said, pointing to Kate.

"Well, you were," said Kate angrily. "You and Ruben were arguing over that worthless Viking junk down in the tunnels."

"It is not worthless," said Teemu.

"Is it worth a human life?" demanded Kate.

"I did not kill him!" cried Teemu.

"That piton belongs to you!"

"Kate, anyone could have used it," said Sarah.

"I did not use that . . . I did not put that there," Teemu said. "Anyone could have taken a Viking Claw from the supply sack."

"Why do you think Teemu did this?" asked Uncle Stoppard.

"I don't know what to think," said Kate.

"They were arguing about the Tquuli treasure," explained Sarah. "Kate told me last night. When we were measuring those bones, the two men got into a big argument. Teemu didn't think Ruben should give ice cubes Viking names."

"It is disrespectful," said Teemu.

"And he thought bringing camera crews up here would also be disrespectful."

"Maybe it was Ice Flo's," I said.

Kate aimed her bleary eyes at me. "Spies, you mean? That was my husband's idea. But I think he was being paranoid."

"But didn't he say they followed him before?" I said. "On other expeditions. Like the one in Bolivia?"

Kate shot a glance at Sarah, then said, "Let's not talk about that right now."

"Why is Ruben's body in that tent?" asked Sarah.

I remembered the blood. Last night I had assumed it was Ruben's blood in the tunnel. If it was, though, that would mean he was killed down in the tunnel. Why drag his lifeless body back up here and zip it inside one of the Jokkipunkis' tents?

Because it would be the last place to look for it. It made sense, if Teemu really had killed Roobick. Only Teemu or Hrór would go inside those tents. That would mean Hrór was in on the killing. Was that possible? He was just a teenager, like me. Hrór should have been sleeping in that tent last night. Unless he stayed away, deliberately making room for the dead body. Hmmm. Hrór in the empty tent.

"Let's radio for help," said Uncle Stoppard.

He certainly was obsessed about using that radio.

Teemu shouted, "It's gone!"

"What?"

"The radio was in that tent last night."

"You're just saying that," said Kate.

"No, I kept it in that tent."

"You're hiding it. You don't want the authorities to know what happened."

"I want them to find my brother," said Teemu.

"Do you?" said Kate accusingly. "Or did you kill him, too?"

Teemu's voice was low and dangerous. "I did not kill my brother. Whoever did kill him will earn my vengeance. And whoever stabbed your husband took that radio."

"Kate, try to calm down," said Sarah.

"Maybe they threw it over the cliff," I said.

"Let's look for it," said Uncle Stoppard. "Finn and I will look over by the eastern ridge. Hrór and Teemu can look west. And Kate and Sarah search the cliffs."

"Yes, yes," said Kate. She took a few deep breaths. "That's a good idea. Come on, Sarah, let's go look. I need to walk."

Great idea. It would keep everyone out of camp, and away from my sleeping bag.

Uncle Stoppard and I walked toward the eastern ridge of rocks.

"Did you hear what Teemu said?" I asked.

"Which part?" said Uncle Stoppard.

"When he talked about Edo. As if he already knew Edo was dead."

"Yes, I noticed that, too."

"Do you think he is? Dead, I mean. Uncle Stoppard? Uncle Stop?"

I saw the footprints.

"Look," said Uncle Stoppard.

It was the *Peephole* photo come to life. My eyes got woozy looking at it. A set of footprints marching across the snowy field—and ending abruptly in mid-stride.

16
Blood Relatives

A long, metal object lay in the snow next to the footprints. I walked over and carefully picked it up.

"A flashlight," I said. The glass lens was cracked.

"Whose is it?" asked Uncle Stoppard.

I glanced at the bottom of the barrel. It was number 7. Climbing expeditions keep strict account of their supplies. Your life may depend on having the correct amount of ropes or pitons or batteries or food. With the double expedition funded by both Uncle Stoppard and Roobick's Cubes, everything must be checked and verified. If we paid for ten flashlights, there had better be ten flashlights.

We had each been assigned a number along with our backpacks, sets of crampons, helmets, and so forth. Personal supplies were tracked by checking our number written on the supplies. Number 7 was Edo.

"He was up here," breathed Uncle Stoppard.

"Let's get our axes and dig," I said. "That's how I found out where my parents' footprints went. Maybe there's another doorway." Thor supposedly had five hundred and forty, right?

We yelled and hollered and waved our arms, getting the others' attention. Then we dug in that field for an hour. Two hours. None of us thought about stopping for breakfast. The ice chips scattered beneath the attack of our axes and shovels. We dug through snow, ice, and crystallized lava. We punctured several layers of rock in some places. We probably destroyed, without knowing it, dozens of delicious streaks and strands of ice that the former Ice Cube King would have given his eyeteeth to taste. But we found no doorway, no sign of Edo Jokkipunki anywhere. We had wasted valuable time. Hours that I could have spent searching for my parents.

Hrór looked at Teemu wearily, then walked back to the campsite.

"Let's get something to eat," said Sarah, putting an arm around Kate's shoulders. "We could all use some breakfast. It's lunchtime now, by my watch."

As we trudged back, I heard Kate say, "Ruben would want me to continue this work. I can't give up the Viking flavors now. Maybe we can even have some kind of memorial service for him up here."

Uncle Stoppard said, "That was a good idea you had, Finn, about digging. But unfortunately, the footprints are now obliterated."

"You think we missed a clue?" I asked.

"Those footprints," he said. "Anyone could have made them."

"What do you mean?"

"All boots make the same kind of marks in the snow," he said. "Apart from yours and Hrór's which are the smallest, and mine which are the largest, they all look pretty much alike."

"But how did they disappear?"

Whoever made the prints didn't go *down*, like my

parents had. They didn't go up into the sky. They stopped going forward, so—

"Someone walked *backward*," I said. "If anyone could have made them, maybe they walked out into the middle of the field, stopped, and then walked *backward*, restepping into the same prints."

Uncle Stoppard smiled. "You must get your genius from my side of the family."

"From watching the little kids at school play Fox and Geese," I said. When there's lots of white stuff on the ground, Minnesota kids stamp a large circle in the snow. Then they divide the circle, like a big pie, into four sections, using two straight lines. One kid is the fox who chases the others, the geese, using those paths to walk in. Either across the straight line paths, or the curving outside circle path. If a kid accidentally runs out of the circle, because he gets nervous or excited, he has to retrace his steps and come back into the established paths. I don't know how many times I've seen someone walk backward in the snow, leaving one set of tracks. When it comes to deciphering clues left in snow, it's hard to fool a Minnesotan.

"You don't think it was goblins, then?" asked Uncle Stoppard. "Or the revenge of a ghostly Viking?"

I remembered how Hrór had laughed yesterday when I mentioned goblins. "It's a trick," I said. "Like the trick played on Goblin Wall."

That phrase in the *Peephole* article came back to me: *As if the Zwakes had been lifted up into the air.* The real explanation for my parents' mysterious footprints was solved not by looking up "into the air," but by looking down. Could Edo's vanishing act also be solved by looking in the opposite direction?

"We need to find that radio before someone is killed," said Uncle Stoppard.

"The blood."

"What?"

"Bloodstains, I found them in the tunnel last night."

"What were you doing in the tunnel?"

"Some last-minute exploring."

We detoured over to the doughnut door.

When we crawled inside, Uncle Stoppard shined his flashlight on the rocky floor.

"Bloodstains," he said.

"Roobick's blood, see?" I asked.

"Or Edo's," he said.

It couldn't be Zwake blood, could it? Too bad we couldn't tell by sight; all blood looks the same to me. In the dim tunnel the spots reminded me of raspberry chocolate. "Let's follow them."

The drops, widely spaced, led us back to the skeleton cavern. The motionless claw still clutched at the boulder. The second skull still grinned at the ceiling.

"Hey! The ring's gone!" I said.

The gold dragon ring was missing from the skeleton's finger bone. In fact, the entire finger had been torn off.

"Someone was down here, all right," said Uncle Stoppard.

Whoever ripped off the skeleton's finger had jostled the skeleton's rib cage. Beneath the skeleton lay another secret. More blood? No, more runes.

"Red lipstick," I said.

"Another message?" asked Uncle Stoppard.

The skeleton had kept anyone from seeing it right away. I shivered a bit, thinking how we narrowly missed it ourselves. The ring thief had done us a favor. I pulled out my journal again, opening to the page with the rune alphabet. I copied the message that Mom or Dad had scrawled in lipstick, and then translated it from the runes into the normal, human alphabet.

MIKILLVEGGUR

"Is that someone's name?" asked Uncle Stoppard. "Finn? Finn?"

I was busy looking at another part of the journal. Dad had listed the names of the other archeologists who would join him and Mom in Iceland. I had whipped through the names once, on the plane, but I had never paid close attention to them. Until now.

Gunnar Gunnarson
Helga Johansdottir
Hrolf Magnusson
Hallur Bjorklund

Dad also recorded where each scientist came from.

"Look at this," I said to Uncle Stoppard. "This guy here came from Myvatn."

"Hrolf Magnusson?"

"Yeah," I said. "Hrór's from Myvatn, too. He told me yesterday. Myvatn is also where some of the trackers came from who looked for Mom and Dad. And—Hrór's dad's name is Hrolf."

"You think that's his father?" asked Uncle Stop.

"You told me that Icelanders don't always have the same last name when they're in the same family,"

I said. "It goes by the first name. See? Hrór Hrolfson?"

Two days ago, when I (and Uncle Stoppard) had discovered the door leading into the tunnel, Uncle Stoppard had blabbed about it back at camp. Hrór had jumped up and said "Parents!" I thought he had been talking about *my* parents. I wondered what would get him so excited about the Zwake family. He mentioned parents again when we spoke by the cliff edge last night. We talked about missing family members. I mentioned Edo, and Hrór said "parents." Naturally, I thought he was thinking of mine. That's why we were up on this mountain anyway, to find them, right? Now I realized Hrór was thinking of his own parents. His father, Hrolf Magnusson, had disappeared at the Thorsnafli along with everyone else who worked in the original Zwake expedition.

Back in his home town, Midge Lake, I wondered if Hrór was ever teased about the Hrolfson Curse? Or the Magnusson Curse?

"Hrolf is a common name in Iceland," said Uncle Stoppard.

"Not that common," said a voice. Hrór snapped on his flashlight; he was standing a few yards away.

"Oh, I didn't hear you," I said.

"Are you all okay, Hrór?" asked Uncle Stoppard.

"You are right," said Hrór, facing me. "Hrolf Magnusson was my father. I mean, *is* my father. He disappeared here at Thorsnafli with your parents, and with his friends."

"You've been up here before," I said.

Hrór nodded. "Two other times I came up with Edo and Teemu. We never found anything. No one thought to look under the snow before you did."

Speaking of looking under, I gazed down at the runes which had been hidden beneath the skeleton's rib cage. "Do you know runes?" I asked.

Hrór stepped beside me and looked at the lipstick message. "Mmm, just a little. But I don't recognize—"

"I wrote it down clearer," I said, showing him my journal.

"Ah, yes," said Hrór. *"Mikillveggur.* That is modern Icelandic, even though the writer used the old runes to spell it."

Clever Mom.

"What does it mean?" I asked Hrór.

"Well, *mikill* means big, huge, great. And *veggur* is a wall or barrier."

Great? Barrier? What was Mom trying to tell us?

"Is that blood?" asked Hrór.

"Yes, we think it belongs to Ruben Roobick," I said.

"Why did you come down here, Hrór?" asked Uncle Stoppard.

"I, uh, came to help," he said. His foxy green eyes darted back toward the entrance of the tunnel.

"The drops lead to the wall over there," I said.

"A dead end," said Hrór.

I flashed my light. A dark ridge of red rock bulged out from the wall. It was where Ruben got his hand steamed. Uncle Stoppard and Hrór turned back, shining their beams along other sections of the cavern, searching for more blood drops. I walked to the jagged ridge. Solid rock. My beam spotted another blood drop on the far side of the ridge. As I stepped around the rock, I noticed a fissure in the wall behind it. A fissure that blended in with the shadows, looking like another shadow itself. Is that where the steam came from? It was narrow, but large enough for a man to squeeze through.

I led the three of us into the crack. Soon the passageway widened and expanded; Uncle Stoppard was able to straighten up. This tunnel was not like the others. First, the air was frosty cold. Secondly instead of traveling in long, straight stretches though the rock, the new tunnel zigzagged into the heart of the mountain. My heart beat faster at the thought of what—or who— might be waiting for us at the other end.

"Was your father looking for Tquuli, too?" I asked Hrór.

"He did not believe in Tquuli," said Hrór. "He thought it was a *fata morgana.*"

"A faded what?"

"*Fata morgana*, an optical illusion," explained Hrór. "Sometimes in the mountains of Iceland, with sunlight pouring on the snow, people see things. False things. Sometimes they see whole cities and mountains that do not exist. It is all a trick of the light."

A mirage. I had seen one of those in the Sahara Desert.

"If he thought Tquuli was an illusion, then why did he come here?"

"He thought Ogar Blueaxe might have been a real person. There are historical records of Vikings attacking Italian treasure ships. He came here with your parents hoping to find evidence proving the story," said Hrór.

"And maybe find gold, too?" I said.

"He did not hunt for gold like some people."

Like who? I wondered.

"The blood drops are getting fatter," said Uncle Stoppard.

The twisty tunnel sloped upward.

"Finn, what time is it?" asked Uncle Stoppard.

I consulted my father's wristwatch. "Almost two o'clock," I answered.

Two o'clock? Something important happened at two o'clock. I could see a giant clock face in a cobwebby corner of my mind. What was my brain trying to tell me? Dad's watch had been frozen at nine o'clock when we discovered it on the skeleton's wrist. Two o'clock was more important. A trick, a deadly trick.

The tunnel zigzagged for a hundred more feet, then opened into a mammoth cavern, larger than the cave holding the two skeletons. At the mouth of the tunnel we paused. Our flashlight beams picked out a vast crowd of heads.

"Tquuli," I breathed.

17
Tquuli

Dragon heads.

They curved up from the prows of ships, their swanlike necks ending in terrible jaws and flashing eyes of wood and iron and bone. The eyes all stared in the same direction, the dragon nostrils all smelled the same invisible wind. A fleet of Viking ships met our gaze, seven or eight, each ship anchored on a pedestal of rock.

"Drakkars," said Hrór. "Dragon ships."

Dad's research notes suggested that Tquuli might be a cemetery. We had found a graveyard of ships.

"Amazing," said Uncle Stoppard.

"Over there," said Hrór. He aimed his flashlight. The blood led farther down. We followed a ramp carved into the rock, sloping to the cavern floor.

"These boats are huge," said Uncle Stoppard. The longest ships ran seventy or eighty feet long. The dragon heads, frozen in an ancient race, rose twenty feet into the cold, dark air. Standing among those huge wooden ships, I felt like a mouse in a maze. Narrow alleys ran alongside and between the ships.

"Hey, Hrór, help me up the side," I said.

Hrór laced his fingers, hoisted my boot, and boosted me up the side of a ship.

"Finn, careful. That ship is ancient," warned Uncle Stoppard.

"It looks like it's in great shape," I said, clambering over the side and dropping down into the hull. Wow! Golden shields hung along both inside walls of the ship. Between every two shields stood a bright spear and sword, pointing to the dark ceiling. The narrow floor was smothered in trunks and chests and small silver boxes.

"I think I see a mummy," I said.

Hrór and Uncle Stoppard had joined me inside the dragon ship.

A dark figure lay in the middle of the ship, draped with an ancient woven tapestry. A shield and spear lay over the top of the tapestry. A real live dead Viking.

"Don't touch him, Finn. It might just dissolve, it's so old."

"You think Ogar Blueaxe killed this guy?" I asked.

"Who knows? But I doubt if Ogar and his single crew hauled all of these boats up here by themselves. It would take half an army."

"There might be a body in each boat," I said.

"They're called ships."

"Hey, a game," said Hrór. He had found a small golden board, covered with rows of dimples. A number of the dimples held round glass beads.

"Marbles," I said. "Or Chinese Checkers."

"More like Viking Checkers," said Uncle Stoppard.

"Think that would fit in our suitcase?"

"Let's check out another one, Finn," said Hrór. He scrambled over the side and dropped down to the cavern floor.

"Finn!" he yelled. I leaned over the side of the ship

and looked down. Hrór was leaning against the hull. His flashlight shook as he pointed at a dark lump on the ground. Another flashlight. This one was stenciled with the number 3. Ruben Roobick. The hair stiffened on the back of my head.

Ruben Roobick had been killed in Tquuli.

"How did he find this place?" I said.

"He must have found it when he explored the main cave," said Hrór. "When we were checking out the skeletons."

"And he didn't tell us," said Uncle Stoppard.

"That steam vent," I said. "I'll bet he saw the tunnel leading here when he got steamed. Then he made up that story about being depressed and disappointed with the cave. He was hoping none of us would find the tunnel. That we'd give up."

"He must have been sweating that day," said Hrór. "When we were all exploring the tunnels, he stayed outside and looked for ice."

"Listen," I whispered.

Footsteps. And the three of us were standing still.

"Turn off your flashlights," Hrór said.

The darkness was incredible. I felt wrapped inside a black velvet sleeping bag. A light twinkled. Someone was walking down the tunnel toward the cave.

Uncle Stoppard and I crept the length of the dragon ship toward its rear end—stern, I think it's called. I couldn't see the glimmering light through any chinks in the old boat, er, ship. Those Vikings sure knew how to make things seaworthy.

I peered over the edge of the hull. The light grew brighter as the steps grew louder.

"It must be the killer," I said. "Whoever killed Roobick knows how to find this place."

I almost screamed when Hrór touched my shoulder.

"Sorry," he said. "I thought I'd join you in here."

"That's okay," I said.

. . . *tick . . . tick . . .*

Dad's watch ticked loudly in the silence. I switched on my beam. Two-twenty.

"Careful, Finn!"

"No one can see through the sides," I said. "How long do you think these ships have been here?"

"Centuries," said Uncle Stoppard.

"Why do they look so new?"

"The cold air must help preserve them," he said. It was cold, all right. We could see our breaths in the cavern.

I rubbed my hands together. I glanced at the watch again. Two twenty-one.

Roobick was dead. Edo was gone. Edo had played a trick. . . .

. . . *trick . . . clock . . .*

Two o'clock!

I knew how Edo had played that trick. How he vanished off the side of the Goblin Wall. Of course, how simple. A magician's trick. We had all been looking in the wrong direction. Staring one way, like the dragon heads, when we should have looked in the opposite direction. Two o'clock.

"Hrór," I said. "You know what happened to Edo, don't you?"

"I don't know how he—no, what do you mean?"

"I mean how he disappeared. How he vanished off the Goblin Wall."

"No."

"You know, Hrór. Hiding a dead body makes you an accessory to murder."

"Finn, what are you talking about?" said Uncle Stoppard.

We sat in the darkness for a few seconds. *"Ja,"* said Hrór. "I know how he did it."

"How Edo vanished?" said Uncle Stoppard, goggling.

"A magic trick," I said. "David Copperfield says it all the time. Magicians force you to look in one place, when the trick is being played in another."

"And the trick was . . .?"

"Remember how I told you that we were like bugs on a clock?"

"While we were camping on the Goblin Wall," Uncle Stoppard said.

"Yeah. I said that you and I were at the center of the clock. I even made a map of where each of us was hanging for my journal."

"The Roobicks were nine o'clock," he said. "And—"

A scrape against rock. The killer? The sound came from the mouth of the tunnel.

Uncle Stoppard placed his finger against his lips, cautioning us to stay silent. The three of us cocked our ears like dogs. Another tiny scrape. A boot on the ramp? With the huge wooden barriers of the Tquuli ship surrounding us, it was difficult to tell where the second scrape came from.

"I have one more question, Hrór," I whispered. "You know how Edo vanished from the Goblin Wall. Do you who know who killed Roobick?"

"I was not here," said Hrór. "I was with you. How could I know who murdered Mr. Roobick?"

"This morning Teemu said that he would avenge your cousin's death. Edo's dead, isn't he?" I said.

"No, I do not know."

A scrape, a loud one at the base of the nearby dragon ship. A figure was walking only a few feet away, separated from us by the thin wooden hull. The footsteps stopped. I thought my lungs would burst. Then the figure moved on, the steps growing fainter in the darkness. We waited and waited.

"We need to follow them," I said.

"Finn, we should return to camp. Look for the radio and call for help."

"Uncle Stoppard, I have the radio. Okay? But we have to follow that person."

"You have the radio?"

"We have to find out who the killer is, or else the rescue team will keep us off this mountain for months with some stupid investigation."

"Why did you take the radio?"

"For voices."

"Voices?"

"Teemu told Roobick he heard Edo's voice, remember? Well, I thought the radio might . . . transmit other voices, too."

"Your parents," said Hrór.

"Yeah, I thought maybe they were nearby. Like Edo. Trapped inside the mountain or something, and trying to call for help."

"I can't believe you stole that radio, Finn."

"I'm sorry," said Hrór. "But Teemu was not telling the truth."

"What?"

"He never heard Edo's voice. He just said that to make Roobick think he was afraid of being up here."

"To soak him for more money," said Uncle Stoppard.

"More money, *ja.*"

No voices?

"We have to follow that person," I said. "If we nab the killer, then we can stay up here on the mountain. We found Tquuli. We can find my parents, too." I stuffed my flashlight back in my jacket, grabbed the boat's side with both hands, and hurled myself over the side.

18
Flying Treasure

The bouncing ball of light, the beam from the killer's flashlight, danced thirty or forty feet ahead of me. Bright enough for me to follow and not collide against a resting dragon ship, but not bright enough to reveal its owner. I tried to time my steps with the killer, my boots scraping against the rock when those boots ahead of me also scraped. I didn't want that flashlight to suddenly spin around and aim at me.

The cavern grew lighter. The figure turned at the end of the passage and slipped behind a wall of rock. Pale gray sunlight trickled in through a fissure ahead of the ships.

This must be the other entrance that Sarah guessed about. The way in for the ships.

Monster icicles, like giant glass teeth, barred the mouth of a tunnel leading outside. Beyond the frozen waterfall, the shadow of the moving figure wavered like a black flame. A drift of snow powdered the floor of the entrance. Following the figure's footprints—there were several trails of prints—a path led behind the icicle teeth and out beneath the blazing blue Icelandic sky. Twenty yards beneath the fissure sat a narrow snowy ledge, a miniature version of the Thorsnafli, and below the ledge slanted the familiar slope of the Thorsfell, a tilting landscape of snow and rock leading hundreds of feet down to the grassy lowlands. A Viking ship rested on the snowy ledge. Smaller than the mega-dragonships within the cavern, the ship ran about six-teen feet long. I figured the sleek wooden sides came up to my mandible. It was exactly the kind of small ship that Sarah had in mind when she talked about Ogar's treasure. This hidden mouth, shielded by ice and snow, was a perfect entryway for Ogar and Skuld and whoever else had buried their ships and treasure and friends inside the mountain.

Standing above the snowy ledge, I saw a body laid out in the Viking ship, draped with a tapestry like the one I'd seen inside. A pair of velvety eyebrows rested beneath a golden metal helmet glittering with rubies and emeralds. Gloves of gold and leather encased the motionless hands, crossed over his chest, lying on top of the rich tapestry. The rest of the ship was filled to the brim with golden coins and plates and weapons.

"Why did you kill him?" I cried.

The figure below me, walking toward the ship, turned to face me.

"I didn't kill him," said Teemu. "But I intend to give him a proper burial."

Something metal flashed in Teemu's fist.

"What about Roobick?" I said.

"He deserved to die," said Teemu grimly.

"Teemu!"

I turned and saw Hrór and Uncle Stoppard stand-ing just outside the cave.

Hrór shouted, "He knows what happened to Edo."

"What do you mean?" asked Teemu.

"The Goblin Wall."

"Ah," said Teemu. "You figured out the trick."

"I know how," I said. "But I don't know why you did it."

"It was money, wasn't it, Teemu?" said Uncle Stoppard.

"You Americans think everything is solved by money," said Teemu. "If the Americans think we poor, superstitious Icelanders are afraid, want to climb down the mountain, they will pay us more money. Other people would have turned back, become frightened. Maybe believed they were not supposed to get to this mountain. But you Americans just spend more money. Two thousand more dollars a day Roobick would have paid us." Teemu shook his head. "He should have turned back."

"Did Roobick figure out the trick, too?" I asked.

"He figured something was going on," said Teemu. "He came down in the tunnels last night, heard Edo and, well, then it was all over."

"Edo found Tquuli, then," I said.

Teemu nodded. "Roobick came down here last night for some last-minute exploring. Edo came down here when the rest of us were in our sleeping bags. He figured that was the only safe time he could do his own exploring. He was so excited about discovering Tquuli. He and I have dreamed about Viking treasure ever since we were young boys. Hrór's age, or younger even. When you found the door leading down here"—he looked at me—"Edo left the tent and followed us. He was too impatient to wait. He thought the risk of being discovered outweighed the joy of discovery."

That was the extra flashlight I saw. Edo was behind the others when they entered the skeleton cave.

"Edo was hiding in your tent?" asked Uncle Stoppard.

"Ja, vist," said Teemu.

"That's how they did the trick in the first place," I said. "When Edo disappeared from the Goblin Wall, he was actually hiding in Teemu and Hrór's tent. I'm sure it was uncomfortable, but they squeezed him in."

"Edo climbed up there in the night?" said Uncle Stoppard.

"Yeah, it was a full moon so he had plenty of light. And when we saw the empty tent the next morning, that's what yanked our attention like a magnet. We were looking at six o'clock, and not at two o'clock, Teemu's tent."

"Nice acting, Hrór," said Uncle Stoppard.

"Yes, he was good," said Teemu.

"I had to do it," said Hrór. "They made me promise."

Hrór had climbed down into Edo's tent and over to the supply sack. He had acted surprised and confused the whole time even though he knew Edo was safely curled up in the other neon-green tent. More than the empty tent and abandoned harness, it was Hrór's sincerity that convinced us Edo had truly vanished from the wall.

"How did Edo get back up the cliff?" said Uncle Stoppard.

"He stayed in the tent," I said. "When we hauled the hammocks and stuff over the cliff edge, we were hauling Edo as well. Remember, you thought he might be hiding in the equipment sack? We forgot to look in the opposite direction, at the other tent."

"Your scheme worked, Teemu," said Uncle Stoppard. "I never suspected Hrór would trick us. He always seemed so honest. But it seems he can be just as deceptive as his older cousins."

"He's a quick learner," said Teemu.

I couldn't blame Hrór, like Uncle Stoppard did. I knew how Hrór felt, that he would do anything to find his dad.

"You did this to keep us from climbing the mountain?" asked Uncle Stoppard. "To frighten us away?"

"Not you, Roobick," Teemu replied.

"What happened to Roobick anyway?" asked Uncle Stoppard. His breath was coming in short, swift gasps.

"He killed Edo," said Teemu. "When Edo had not come back from the tunnels, it was getting late. I climbed into the tunnels and followed him here. He and I dragged this ship outside. If we could, we would drag each one with our bare hands and shove them down the mountainside rather than let Roobick find them and put them in one of his godless commercials. But then he came down to the tunnels last night for more exploring, too. He heard us moving the ship. Roobick realized we had tricked him. He threatened to tell the authorities, take away our licenses. But he thought we were just doing it for the gold. That's all *he* could understand."

"So he killed Edo accidentally?" I said.

"There are no accidents," said Teemu. "Everything happens for a reason. Edo and Roobick fought. Roobick . . . hit him with his flashlight."

What about Edo's flashlight?

"Did you make those phony footprints, too?" I said.

"We made them last night, after you went to bed. Before Edo went in the tunnels."

More spooky stuff to frighten the Roobicks, or at least to give the Icelanders another reason for leaving Thor's Mountain.

"How exactly did Roobick die?" asked Uncle Stoppard.

During this whole conversation, Teemu had edged closer to the Viking treasure. Without realizing it, Uncle Stop and Hrór and I had also moved down the slope and nearer Edo's funeral ship.

Teemu looked nervously at Hrór. Was he worried what Hrór might think of him? Was he afraid of losing his young cousin's respect, his admiration?

"If I had not avenged my brother, I would bring shame to my family."

"Your family's not ashamed of murder?" I said.

Teemu ignored me. "I laid Edo's body inside the ship. I would give him a true Viking burial. Roobick's body was left in the cave where it fell. I did not put it in the tent."

Yeah, right. And you didn't stab him with the Viking Claw, either, I thought.

"So who did put Roobick's body there?"

"It was a message to me," said Teemu. "Someone knew I killed Roobick. They were laying the guilt at my doorstep. Seeing what I would do."

Kate or Sarah must have seen him kill Roobick. This morning one of them pretended to see the body for the first time. Which woman? Unless there was another person on the mountain. A spy from Ice Flo's? Freya?

"But you did it," I said. "You killed him."

Teemu nodded. "I struck back at him. Revenge for Edo's death."

Hrór remained silent next to Uncle Stoppard.

The metal object flashed in Teemu's hand again. A lighter. He was going to set the ancient tapestry on fire. That dry old rug would blaze like a pile of leaves. If Edo died in the burning Viking ship, evidence would be destroyed as well. Along with the treasure my parents came here to find. Edo's body needed to remain intact. The authorities needed it to prove that Uncle Stoppard and I had nothing to do with the murders on Thor's Mountain, so we would be allowed to stay up here and continue our search.

CLANG!

I swiped a gold sword from the ship and struck the lighter, sending it spinning down the snowy slope.

"Good one, Finn!" said Uncle Stoppard.

A loud metallic roar echoed across the snowy ledge. The clanging grew. The roar was followed by a low rumble. Uncle Stoppard and I looked up. A huge drift of snow lay above the frozen waterfall entrance. The drift was almost as large as the entire Thorsnafli.

"Careful," whispered Teemu. "You don't want to cause an avalanche, do you?"

He grabbed another sword from the ship's treasure. The two of us swung at each other with the ancient weapons. The huge gold blades shivered through the air, morning sunlight gleaming in watery lines across Edo's tapestry. The light sometimes shone right in my eyes. I hadn't thought to wear my goggles in the tunnel.

Where was Uncle Stoppard? I couldn't look around. I had to keep my eyes on Teemu's deadly blade. All this because he wanted to bury his brother in some ancient Viking ritual? Woof! Teemu's sword suddenly swooped down, almost connecting with my neck. What do you call a headless Popsicle? An opsicle?

CLANG!

The swords collided with a terrific roar. Teemu turned swiftly and grabbed a shield from the ship's side. What was that second roar? Teemu and I both staggered in the snow.

The drift of snow above the waterfall rumbled like an awakening beast. Crackles ripped through the air, like Freya popping her own bubble wrap. Powdery snow shimmered down across the icicle mouth.

"Look up!" I cried. A huge wedge of snow was cracking off from the main drift. It would fall directly on top of us.

"Into the boat!" yelled Uncle Stoppard.

I dived into the ship, headfirst, sinking beneath the sea of gold coins.

Uncle Stoppard grabbed hold of the side of the treasure ship. He pushed as if he were trying to free a car trapped in a Minnesota snowbank, the veins standing out on his forehead.

"Get in! Get in!" I shouted.

The treasure ship was slipping forward. Uncle Stoppard leaped aboard. "Hold on!" he cried. "This is gonna be a bumpy ride!"

"Where's Hrór?" I yelled. I looked back and saw Hrór racing back to the mouth of the cave. Please let him get inside in time!

The treasure ship gathered speed, following the natural slope of the mountainside.

BAARRRROOOOM! The wedge of snow crashed into the slope directly behind us. The avalanche thrust cold clouds of billowing snow against our

heads, our shoulders, and the ship. The ship plummeted forward faster.

The angle of our ride was not one I was completely
comfortable with. It was steeper than the roller
coaster in the Mall of America. And a lot faster. And
a lot longer. The ship skimmed over the snow of the
Thorsfell, cold air whipping past our ears, gold coins
scattering into the wind. Why did I have to be the
one sitting in the front?

"What—happens—when—we—run—out—of—
snow?" I stuttered

"I think we're already there," said Uncle Stoppard.

We braced ourselves against the sides of the ship.
The ancient wood and leather scraped over the hard-
ened lava flow. Where was Teemu?

"Look!" cried Uncle Stoppard.

Teemu was glissading down the slope, using his
shield as a snow saucer. Oops! The saucer struck a
bump and sent Teemu rocketing over the ship. I
glanced up the slope and saw the avalanche growing;
more of the drift was breaking up, bigger clouds pur-
sued our ship. I should have brought my safety helmet!
Oh wait—I grabbed a gold-and-leather helmet from
the piles of treasure around me and fastened it on my
head.

"Uncle Stoppard! Put on Edo's helmet!" I yelled.
Edo wasn't going to need it.

"Good idea."

He pulled off the golden helmet, and Edo's eyebrows fluttered.

"Roobick," he said.

I think Uncle Stoppard screamed. Edo sat up in
the quaking ship, the gold coins sliding past him, his

legs caught in the crumbling tapestry. "Where am I?"
he said.

The boat ripped across the lava slopes. Sections of
the hull tore off. Wood splinters flipped into the air.
Grindings and creakings screamed in our ears.
Goblets and shields flew out of the ship and banged
across the mountainside, a shower of gold following
in our wake as we plummeted downward.

The back third of the ship was cracking, splitting
off. Uncle Stoppard threw himself forward, grabbed
my feet, and pulled himself to my side of the hull.
The two of us pulled Edo forward, settling him
between us. More and more treasure slid and rico-
cheted out of the ship. The avalanche tumbled
behind us. Since the ship was growing smaller and
lighter, it raced forward even faster.

Below us, at the foot of the mountain, I spied a tiny
purple box. Freya's chariot. Oh, no, the nuns were in
the direct path of our ship. They were staring up the
mountain. They saw us. I saw them see us. One of the
nuns, grape-sized, ran to the miniature van. It slowly
backed up. Hurry! I thought. Get out of the way!

The van turned around, the rest of the grapes
jumped inside, then it took off.

A horrible ripping sound, as if the world were tear-
ing in half, shuddered through the countryside.
Slowly, slowly, the treasure ship—the remaining two-
thirds of it—skidded roughly to a halt.

Half the gold was gone.

"Are you all right?" A motherly looking woman in
a purple robe bent over me.

"Finn! Finn!" murmured Uncle Stoppard. One of
the nuns turned to her sister and said, "I think
they're from Finland."

I took a long, deep breath. These were not the same nuns who had given us a ride to the mountain base camp. It was a separate chapter. "We're from Minnesota," I said.

"Ah, Minnesota." A third nun nodded. "Yes, yes. Isn't that where Mona Trafalgar-Squeer lives?"

19
Freya's Mountain

The helicopters swung over the gleaming crown of the Thorsfell.

"There's Thorsnafli," I pointed.

The copter pilot gave me the thumbs-up and guided his bird toward the tiny ledge far below us.

Teemu had lied about helicopters not being able to fly to Thor's Belly Button. Just another lie to keep us isolated, victims to his and Edo's campaign to frustrate the Roobicks, while at the same time helping Uncle Stoppard and me (and Hrór) find Tquuli. Now Teemu was lying again. This time lying in a hospital in Reykjavik. He had avoided being buried alive in the avalanche, but had fractured his left wrist, suffered a minor concussion, and broken a humerus. I forget which one. He lost the gold saucer shield beneath the snow.

Uncle Stoppard and Edo and I were all treated for concussions. Edo also had frostbite.

The next day we contacted the local search-and-rescue teams. Teemu had only pretended to radio them from the mountain. Uncle Stoppard and I were allowed to fly with them to the Thorsfell. On the TV screen in my brain, I kept replaying the same scene over and over. Hrór running back to the mouth of the icicle cave as the building-size blocks of snow toppled toward him.

I kept replaying another image in my head: the headline of the article that Sarah O'Hara picked up on the floor of the Hotel Puffin lobby: BOLIVIAN ICE-CUBE EXPEDITION ENDS IN TRAGEDY. Two years ago a team of ice explorers from Roobick's Cubes had traveled to the mountains near Bolivia's Lake Poopo. I was pretty sure I knew who was on that team.

The helicopter swooped over the campsite. Two figures ran out from their tents and waved at us. The birds set down a hundred feet away from the closest tent.

"Hrór!" I yelled. The red-headed teenager ran to greet me.

"I thought the avalanche—" he started.

"Edo and Teemu are okay," I said.

His face paled. "Edo?"

"He wasn't dead," I said. "Teemu thought he was, but Roobick just knocked him unconscious. They're both in the hospital."

"Will Teemu be arrested?" he asked. Hrór looked suddenly past my shoulder. I turned and saw the Reykjavik police officers climbing out of the copter. Their black boots and jackets stood out like ink against the white snow.

"I don't think so," I said.

Kate ran up to join us. She shook Uncle Stoppard's hand. "We tried radioing for help," she said. "Hrór found the two-way."

"In my—?"

"In the equipment sack," said Hrór, winking at me. "I don't know how it got there."

"It didn't matter," said Kate. "The blasted thing

wouldn't work. We thought the two of us would have to climb down on our own."

"Two of you?"

Kate directed the officers to her husband's body lying in Edo's former tent.

Hrór whispered to me, "I think Teemu took a part out of the radio. No one would be able to operate it except him."

Teemu was clever. He was guilty of a lot of things, but not murder.

"Where is she?" Uncle Stoppard asked Kate.

Kate wrung her gloved hands. "We don't know," she said. "We searched part of the tunnels, but it wasn't easy. Hrór and I did it one at a time. We always wanted to keep one of us out here in case that rescue team showed up."

If Uncle Stop and I hadn't made it down the mountain in Edo's ship, the rescue team would never have arrived. Kate and Hrór would have had to make the dangerous attempt of climbing back down the Thorsfell themselves. What if one of them had fallen into a gas bubble on the way down?

"The Tquuli entrance, where the ships were brought in, is blocked by snow," said Hrór. "So we know she is somewhere in the tunnels. There are no footprints leading anywhere off the ledge."

"But the tunnels are empty," said Kate. "I'm sure I searched every one."

"Why did she do it?" Uncle Stoppard asked.

I knew why, I just didn't know how it happened. Sort of the reverse of the Edo trick. "Sarah was in love with Gomez," said Kate. "And she was always accusing Ruben of getting the team into dangerous situations. Climbing too many hours in the day, crossing over dangerous snow bridges. When Gomez fell into that crevasse down in Bolivia, Sarah and Ruben were both there. She blamed Ruben for the poor man's death. She said she got over it, the accident was behind her, it's been two years now. But I know it always gnawed at her. Ruben was able to forget about it, because that's just the way he is—was—forget about the bad stuff, laugh, and move on with your life. Sarah was not like that."

We reached the doughnut door. The police stayed behind, strapping Ruben Roobick's body into the helicopter carrier.

Down in the tunnels, we traced our flashlights over every inch of rock. We saw the crampon again, the twin skeletons, the rune message written in lipstick on the rock floor.

Sarah had vanished.

In the Tquuli cave, I had to catch my breath again. The dragon ships were beautiful and frightening all at once. This was the ancient treasure that my parents had searched for. Where were they now? We knew they were not on the mountain. I was sure the clues they left behind, the wristwatch and the runes, would tell us their true location. And I think it has something to do with the Ackerberg Institute. After all, the Ackerbergs own helicopters, too.

"Hrór and I have gone over every square inch of this cave," said Kate. "The treasure is magnificent, isn't it? At first I thought the dragon ships should be in a museum somewhere, for other people to enjoy them. But then I thought, this place is a natural museum. These ships belong here."

"Did she tell you what happened?" I asked.

"About Ruben, you mean? She felt terribly guilty.

She left a note for me to read the next morning. But she was gone."

"I read the note," Hrór whispered to me.

"What happened?"

"Sarah got up late that night. She was going to visit Teemu in his tent, but she saw him walking toward the metal door. So she followed him."

Was everyone down in that tunnel? We should have slept down there; it was much warmer than the slope.

"After Teemu pushed Roobick down, Roobick was stunned. He woke up and found himself alone. I guess that's when Teemu was placing Edo in the treasure ship. Sarah came across Roobick and heard what happened. She wrote that his head was bleeding from a wound."

Kate was having a hard time talking. "Maybe Sarah became upset when she saw Ruben like that. Maybe it reminded her of that other time, down in Bolivia, when Ruben got into a fight with Gomez. And then later, Gomez—well, I'm sure you heard all about that."

Kate wiped her eyes.

"Last night, Sarah found herself alone with Ruben," she continued. "They were alone, no one to see them. He was already weak from the fight. She grabbed the first thing she found in her pack, a Viking Claw, and stabbed him. I-I don't think she really knew what she was doing."

"Why did she carry him back to the tent?" I asked.

"She didn't think anyone would look in there. People were exploring all over the tunnels, she thought it wouldn't be safe to leave him there. And in the cold outside, his body would be preserved and wouldn't—you know—"

"Smell?"

"Ja," said Hrór.

I wondered why Edo's body didn't freeze out in the treasure ship overnight. But then, he was covered with the heavy tapestry and the heaps of gold coins for insulation, and he wore that helmet and those thick leather gloves. And he had tough Finnish skin. A regular pit bull.

That gave me a brainstorm.

"I know where she is," I said.

"You do?" said Kate.

"I can't say exactly, but I know she has to be in one of eight places."

"Eight?" said Hrór.

There were eight dragon ships in the Tquuli cave.

Ten minutes later we found her in the fifth ship we searched. The figure in the center of that ship, beneath the burial tapestry, was wider than the others. Two bodies lay side by side. An ancient Viking and an American explorer. A Viking Claw piton lay at her side on the floor of the ship, its tip thick with dried blood where it had slashed across her.

From beneath the tapestry, encircled by a thin modern-day wristwatch, dangled a lifeless human hand, a frozen claw.

A Note from Stoppard Sterling

Alphabet is made up of two Greek words, *alpha* and *beta*, which happen to be the first two letters in that system. The Greeks did not invent the alphabet; they did, however, polish it up for the rest of Western civilization and give it a name. In the same manner, the ancient Runic system is called *futhark*, a word made up of the first six letters of Old Norse: *f, u, th, a, r,* and *k*. For centuries, *futhark* consisted of twenty-four letters. In the ninth century, Ogar Blueaxe's time, the Germanic peoples who used *futhark* went on a drastic reduction program, leaving them with only sixteen letters.

Icelanders love their age-old traditions, but they are not afraid of welcoming change. Recently the Thorsfell volcano was renamed the Freijafell. Hrór Hrolfson was recently honored for his discovery of ancient Viking artifacts in the caves that honeycomb the aforesaid volcano. Iceland has also become the home of the newest distribution center for Roobick's Cubes. Kate Roobick, the new president of Roobick's Cubes, has introduced a new flavor to her company's ever-growing line of ice products, Zwakeberry. I have not tasted it.

My nephew Finnegan has taken quite an interest

in the older Viking traditions, especially runes. He is convinced that the message discovered on the floor of the "skeleton cave" is a clue left behind by his parents. Taken with the other clues, a wristwatch set at nine o'clock, and a red runic *A* scribbled on a Viking mandible, they should determine the actual location of Anna and Leon Zwake. The letter *A* and the Icelandic words meaning "great" and "barrier" have certainly determined where we shall next search for them.

I am still confused by the wristwatch.

About the Author

Michael Dahl, the author of more than a dozen non-fiction books, has also published poetry and plays. A theater director, actor, and comedian in Minneapolis, Dahl has a wide variety of unusual creatures in his household: Venus's-flytraps, fiddler crabs, African dwarf frogs, an elementary school teacher, and an Australian red-heeler named Gus. He can be e-mailed at finnswake@aol.com.

FINNEGAN ZWAKE

THE NEXT
FINNEGAN ZWAKE MYSTERY

THIRTEEN-YEAR-OLD FINNEGAN ZWAKE, HIS UNCLE STOPPARD, A BESTSELLING MYSTERY WRITER, AND THEIR FRIEND JARED ARE OFF TO AN ARCHAEOLOGICAL DIG IN SUNNY AGUALAR, LAND OF GIANT CACTI, JUNGLES, AND DINOSAURS. DEAD ONES, THAT IS.

WHILE FINN AND HIS UNCLE ARE DIGGING UP TREASURE, THE CREW IS DIGGING UP VERY VALUABLE DINOSAUR EGGS. BUT DIGGING TOO DEEPLY CAN STIR UP TROUBLE, NOT TO MENTION A MURDER, OR TWO, OR THREE....

READ

THE WORM TUNNEL
By Michael Dahl

CPSIA information can be obtained at www.ICGtesting.com

235218LV00001B/88/P